"I don't want to put you in danger."

"I *am* in danger, Riley."

His eyes gleamed bitterly. "I don't want to put you in *more* danger, Nina. I don't want to hurt you. I never wanted that." The strain in his voice shook her. "God, Nina, I can't take one step more into this room because I know I'll hurt you again if I do—don't you see that?"

She stepped toward him. "Do you think it hurts me less *not* to know that? To think that you *don't* want me?"

She came to a stop in front of him. She could feel his heat, his need. It crackled like an electrical charge between them.

"You don't need me in your bed, Nina. You're vulnerable. You're in trouble. You need help, not—"

Touching his chest, she felt his heart pounding. "I don't care."

Dear Reader,

November is full of excitement—vengeance, murder, international espionage and exploding yachts. Not in real life, of course, but in those stories you love to read from Silhouette Intimate Moments. This month's romantic selections will be the perfect break from those unexpected snowstorms or, if you're like me, overeating at Thanksgiving (my mother challenges me to eat at least half my body weight). Oh, and what better way to forget about how many shopping days are left until the holidays?

Popular author Marilyn Pappano returns to the line with *The Bluest Eyes in Texas* (#1391), in which an embittered hero wants revenge against his parents' murder and only a beautiful private investigator can help him. *In Third Sight* (#1392), the second story in Suzanne McMinn's PAX miniseries, a D.C. cop with a special gift must save an anthropologist from danger and the world from a deadly threat.

You'll love Frances Housden's *Honeymoon with a Stranger* (#1393), the next book in her INTERNATIONAL AFFAIRS miniseries. Here, a design apprentice mistakenly walks into a biological-weapons deal, and as a result, she and a secret agent must pose as a couple. Can they contain their real-life passion as they stop a global menace? Brenda Harlen will excite readers with *Dangerous Passions* (#1394), in which a woman falls in love with her private investigator guardian. When an impostor posing as her protector is sent to kidnap her, she has to trust that her true love will keep her safe.

Have a joyous November and be sure to return next month to Silhouette Intimate Moments, where your thirst for suspense and romance is sure to be satisfied. Happy reading!

Sincerely,

Patience Smith
Associate Senior Editor

Third Sight

SUZANNE McMINN

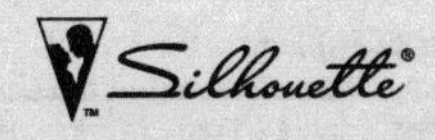

INTIMATE MOMENTS™

Published by Silhouette Books

America's Publisher of Contemporary Romance

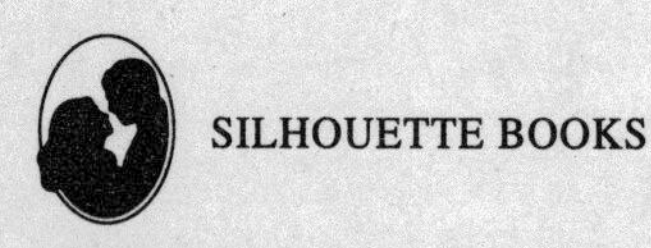

ISBN 0-373-27462-9

THIRD SIGHT

This edition published by arrangement with Harlequin Books S.A.

Visit Silhouette Books at www.eHarlequin.com

Printed in U.S.A.

Books by Suzanne McMinn

Silhouette Intimate Moments

Her Man To Remember #1324
Cole Dempsey's Back in Town #1360
The Beast Within #1377
Third Sight #1392

Silhouette Romance

Make Room for Mommy #220
The Bride, the Trucker and the Great Escape #1274
The Billionaire and the Bassinet #1384

SUZANNE McMINN

lives by a lake in North Carolina with her husband and three kids, plus a bunch of dogs, cats and ducks. Visit her Web site at www.SuzanneMcMinn.com to learn more about her books, newsletter and contests. Check out www.paxleague.com for news, info and fun bonus features connected to her PAX miniseries about paranormal superagents!

With much love to my husband, always.

Chapter 1

She woke in pitch darkness.

Nina Phillips rolled over, gasping at the searing pain caused by the movement. Her head throbbed, and for seconds, she could only focus on taking one breath at a time, her eyes open but blind. She didn't know where she was, didn't know anything but the darkness, nightmarish and unearthly.

Then she registered the cold and with it, her surroundings—the storage rooms housing items not currently on display in the Washington, D.C., Institute of Art and Culture. The rooms were environmentally controlled for the collections' preservation—which meant they were always too cold for her liking. Cold and windowless. And now dark.

Awareness came back to her in dazed increments, and she struggled to order her thoughts. She remembered clicking her security card in the slot, the sound sharp in the stillness of the museum after closing time. She remembered opening the door to Storage Room One. Switching on the light, she'd set down her purse and walked down one of the aisles to the drawered cabinets in the rear, where the El Zarpa stones—ancient, irreplaceable and vital to her research—were kept.

And then she remembered turning, hearing a sound, seeing a shadow near the door, the room plunging into darkness.

Hadn't she shut the door, secured it, behind her?

She was certain she had. She'd worked at the museum, on and off between research expeditions, for nearly ten years. She knew the drill. Security was the top priority. Didn't they repeat that at every staff meeting? And she above all believed in it. Her research—her career as an anthropologist—depended on it.

Especially now.

Yet someone had been there in the storage room. The someone who had turned out the lights.

She remembered shooting pain. Then nothing.

How long had she been out?

Panic crawled up Nina's throat. She sat up, swallowing another gasp of discomfort as fresh pain washed through her temples. She reached for the waistband of her pants, clumsily tore her cell phone from its clipped position. The phone felt dead in her numb fingers, but when she fumbled over the keypad, the display lit.

A sound broke through her focus. Her heart all but tripped over itself.

Then she realized the sound had come from outside the building. Thunder. The spring storm that had been threatening all day was breaking loose.

She pressed the number for help on her cell phone.

"Tremaine."

Emotions smashed into her. She dropped the phone. The clatter of it hitting the concrete floor shattered through her panic. She grabbed the phone back.

"I'm sorry," she breathed hoarsely. "I didn't mean—" Instead of hitting 911, she had simply pressed 1, Riley's number on her speed dial.

She couldn't explain, even to herself, why more than a year later she hadn't deleted it. Or why, when she'd meant to call help, she'd simply, instinctively, pressed 1.

"Nina?"

His voice killed her. Deep, intense, rich with a familiar West Texas drawl. So much—too much—rushed back into her mind, her heart, just from the sexy slide of his voice. Her pulse beat crazily and she struggled to think. It had been thirteen months since they'd broken up, but his image remained fixed in her memory every day, every night—his thick brown hair, straight nose, diamond-cut jaw, eyes caught between blue and black, the casual way he walked, his body filling worn Levi's as if they'd been invented just for him.

"I meant to call the police."

"I *am* the police."

"I meant 911."

"What's wrong?" Riley asked. "Where are you?"

"I'm at the museum."

She wanted to say, *Where do you think I am? What do you think has been my whole life since you left me?*

How quickly the anger tumbled over heartbreak, even in the midst of fear. She worked to shove the emotions away.

"I was just assaulted." She heard something through the wireless connection, like a sharp intake of breath. "I mean, someone hit me on the head, knocked me out."

"I'm in my car and I'm on my way right now. I'm radioing it in to the station just in case there's already a black-and-white closer to the museum than I am. I'll have an ambulance on the way, too. Are you alone?"

Oh, God.

Fear sickened her stomach. What if she wasn't alone? The pitch darkness closed around her with a new menace.

"I don't know," she whispered. She listened so hard, her ears felt as if they were throbbing. "I think so."

"Don't hang up."

She heard him speaking in the background, radioing in the call for police and paramedics, his voice clipped, businesslike. She didn't let herself think about that sharp intake of breath when, for just a second, he might have thought she'd meant another kind of assault. She didn't dare let herself think he cared on any level other than a professional one. She knew better.

Holding the phone, she pushed back with her other arm, feeling her way. She came to her feet, reached out. Her hand struck the compact shelving that lined the aisles of the storage room.

The soft click of the shelving carriage jarring in its steel tracks sounded loud in the eerie dark.

"Nina?"

"I'm still here."

"Don't hang up," he told her again. "I'm almost there."

"How far away are you?" She hated the break in her voice.

"I'm on F Street, near Seventh. Not far. Don't panic."

Too late. "I'm fine," she lied. She wasn't fine, and she wasn't going to feel any better when Riley got there, despite that she wished he were there already.

"Nina, tell me where you are in the museum, exactly."

"Storage Room One. Go around to the rear parking lot, to the guard station. That's the closest entrance to the storage rooms." Security. Her training took over. "I have to press the security Call button." She had to get to the alarm. There was one at every station in the storage rooms.

Why hadn't the alarm gone off if someone had broken in?

"I just can't see—" she whispered.

"Be careful," he said quickly. "You don't know who else could still be there—if not in that storage room, in another. Even if they're gone, they might come back."

"Are you trying to make me feel better? Because if you are, it's not working." She gulped down a half sob, half laugh. She was afraid if she gave in to either, she'd lose her tenuous grip on her self-control.

"I'm trying to save your life. If they were willing to hit you once, they're going to be willing to hit you again. You're better off staying in that room—you don't know what's outside it. Get under something if you can. A desk, a table, any place you can hide. Do you have anything you could use to protect yourself, use as a weapon?"

"I don't know." There were thousands of artifacts in the storage rooms that could be used as weapons; there were, in fact, actual weapons in the stored collections. But they were inside aluminum boxes, padded drawers and covered shelves.

Finding her bearings, her fingertips skimming the steel frameworks of the shelving, she moved, unseeing, toward the back of the storage room, toward the desk. She'd never had a reason to press the alarm before, but she knew there was one under the desk.

She tore open the desk drawer, fumbled for the flashlight she remembered seeing there the last time she'd been in the drawer. Her fingers curled around the hard casing of the flashlight. It was heavy and long.

If she needed it to be, it could be a weapon. She hoped she didn't need it to be.

She flicked the switch. Outside, she heard more thunder, followed by a torrent of rain lashing against the roof high above. Inside, her flashlight beam spread out in a circle, hitting the desktop and the bulletin board over it. Neatly tacked articles covered the board. The headlines read Mysterious El Zarpa Stones Depict Advanced Ancient Society, Anthropologist Uncovers Prehistoric Engraved Records and

Extraordinary Carvings Reveal Lost Civilization. Nina had pinned those stories up herself.

Someone else had left a newspaper on the desk, spread open to a photograph of Nina and a story she would never have cut out. A story she only wished would go away. El Zarpan Government Calls Stones A Hoax, the headline read.

"Nina?"

She jerked her gaze from the headline, and the flashlight's glowing orb spanned the room as she turned, looked up the aisle toward the door. She could see now that it stood barely cracked open. She would never have left it that way.

"I'm still here," she whispered into the phone. "I found a flashlight." She knelt and peered under the desk, lit the switch. "I'm pressing the security Call button." Shaking, she jabbed the red button beneath the research station. She stood, her back to the desk. "I hear a siren."

"That's me. I'm turning into the rear lot."

Through the phone, she heard Riley talking to the guard even as her emergency security call went through to alert them. Her heart pounded into her throat. *What if the assailant was still out there? What if something happened to Riley?*

An emotion she didn't dare name stung her eyes, shot her pulse off the scale. Horribly long moments passed. Then the door burst open and he was in the doorway. New panic arrowed into her, panic of an entirely different kind.

He stood in shadows, but her eyes locked instantly with his. Her breath stalled in her throat. Her heart thudded against her ribs. For a strange moment, she wondered if he was real.

Overhead lights flicked on and uniformed officers, the backup he'd radioed for, came in behind him, fanning out in the room. She could see museum security guards racing through the corridor. The building would be locked down and searched.

Riley came straight to her. In the sudden stark glare, he hardly resembled the man she had loved. He was wet, his dark hair—long enough to curl over his collar—plastered to his head and body from running from his car to the building in the rain. He wore civilian clothes—a leather jacket over a chambray shirt, faded jeans riding down his legs, worn boots covering his feet. But that wasn't what made him seem different. The planes of his face somehow looked more severe, the depths of his lithic eyes more hollow. For just a second, she almost could have sworn his body was now empty of a soul.

What had happened to him in the last thirteen months?

Then he reached her, all six feet plus of him.

There was so much about him that was the same. Lean and dark and all male. The carved shadow of his jaw, the hard-muscled sleekness of his body, the take-charge air of a man others would turn to in a crisis. He was as brilliant as he was intense. He had been so compelling, in fact, that he had overwhelmed her in the six months they'd been together. He'd never said the words she'd wanted to hear, and somehow she'd never noticed. Until it was over

"Nina."

The low, unbearable sexiness of his voice—rousing and irresistible, exuding pure masculine power—slammed through her. And when he smiled, she knew there would be the faintest hint of dimples winking at the corners of his strong mouth.

But he wasn't smiling now.

The bittersweetness of seeing him all but undid her. She had known she wouldn't be able to bear him, and oh, she had been so right. The pain in her head was nothing compared to the burning ache in her heart.

She looked away, desperately, and blinked for an awful beat, needing time to recover, to control her reactions. Delayed recognition of what she was seeing now hit her in waves of shock that broke through the turmoil of emotion.

The wall of cabinet drawers hung open.

The El Zarpa stones were gone.

Chapter 2

Riley saved Nina for last. Not because of his personal feelings for her—he was too professional for that. It was only appropriate that he wait for paramedics to check her over before she made her statement. It was clear she'd been in some kind of shock.

And maybe he was lying to himself about his personal feelings and his professionalism. Even now, from across the room, something moved within him, something deep, but he could, and he would, put it down to something else.

Something, perhaps, even more dangerous.

He'd walked into the storage room and the sensation of energy had nearly knocked him down, the experience had come upon him that quickly.

It had started with a buzzing sensation. Then it had washed over him like a tidal wave, more intense than ever before. Immediately, he'd gone out of his body, to that unknown space where he connected to visions of evil. And yet at the same time, his eyes had registered Nina. Upon seeing her face, he had snapped back, like a taut rubber band, before he could make sense of his dark, deadly sight.

More than a year had passed since the night a seemingly routine call had ended in a car crash that had left him near death with rapidly diminishing brain activity. He'd woken a different man. A man with a new life he'd never planned, and a destiny that couldn't be denied.

He would have died if it hadn't been for the PAX League. They'd saved him, and now they owned him. He remained a police officer—after all, it was the perfect cover. But his true work now lay in the covert world behind the bland exterior of a Washington, D.C., building. It was the world of PAX, Paranormal Allied eXperts. While the public knew the PAX League as an organization dedicated to the philosophical pursuit of global peace through its human rights missions, environmental campaigns and charitable projects, it was in truth nothing more than the shell of a top secret international antiterrorist agency. *Peace through PAX.*

The PAX League had spent years researching the mystical, telepathic, transformational sciences, and he had become the perfect subject for further experimentation. He'd fit the profile they'd been looking for, and PAX had stepped in, whisked him off to a secret clinic where a specialized, deadly chip had been implanted in his brain. He'd gone from near dead to a walking, talking PAX tool.

It had spelled the end of any future he might have had with Nina. And he could only pray now that if evil indeed had laid its hands on the museum this night, it hadn't had anything to do with her, that she had happened to be in the wrong place at the wrong time. It was just a bitter irony that he was the one who'd come to her rescue.

Nina hated him, and she deserved to. He couldn't change the past. The months of separation and grief gathered inside him, and just looking at her hurt.

She was as beautiful as ever, with her cream-skinned face, delicate, with fascinating hollows that belied her strong, athletic body. Her attire was simple—tailored slacks and a white blouse that would be, he knew, more expensive than they looked. The twists of gold at her ears and the jeweled lapel pin were subtle accents revealing her moneyed background as a prestigious senator's daughter. She still had the same proud mossy-green eyes, the same wide, generous mouth, the same heart-shaped facial structure framed by a shoulder-length mist of straight auburn hair. She was thinner, though, and there were dark circles under her eyes. She worked too hard, always had. She hadn't earned her place at the prestigious institute through any familial favor. She'd earned a doctorate in pre-Columbian anthropological studies and become a renowned expert in her field.

She was in trouble these days, though. He'd seen enough in the papers to know that much. Her last South American expedition had yielded a fantastic discovery that had made a media splash—stone tablets from El Zarpan caves, almost comparable to an ancient library of a sophisticated lost civilization. Remarkable images were reported to include medical transplants and blood transfusions, men riding what appeared to be dinosaurs, advanced technology such as telescopes, lost continents and global catastrophes. Suddenly Nina's face had been everywhere—newspapers, magazines, television.

Riley had done his best to avoid the news for months, but he hadn't missed the latest story making headlines now. The government of the small island off the coast of Peru had labeled the find a fraud. The El Zarpan native who had guided Nina into the jungle had admitted to carving the stones himself. Now Nina—and the museum—were the focus of an international firestorm.

Riley had no idea how hard it all had to be on Nina, but he knew she didn't need more trouble—or him. But she had both, at least for tonight. And if he was correctly identifying the force of evil here…

Or were his senses skewed by old feelings for Nina, old feelings that had no place in his new life?

He forced his gaze off Nina, walked around the storage room for the last time. He absorbed every detail, making certain nothing was missed. Flashes of evil pricked at him. Months of recovery and training had prepared him, but he wasn't prepared for Nina. The dark sight reached but couldn't find. Something interfered, tore him in more than one direction.

Nina. Even now, with his back to her, she shook his world. Desire, fear and a dozen other emotions raced through his body, tangling with the focus he knew he required.

He came back around to the front of the room and stopped in front of the museum director, Richard Avano. The security chief, Danny Emery, had accompanied the officers in identifying the specific missing artifacts, which were isolated to the El Zarpa stones. Nina's office also had been entered and her computer hard drive and files relating to the stones stolen.

Detectives had collected and labeled what little evidence there was to be found—fingerprints that might simply belong to museum personnel and all rolling security tapes.

"Our alarms are monitored twenty-four hours a day," Avano said. "They signal locally as well as at the police dispatch station. We have programmable access employing digital and biometric readers. Every door in this building is alarmed and recorded. There are cameras on all exterior and public access areas. We have systems that alarm to signal tampering. What the hell went wrong? How could someone get into the museum, steal the stones and attack Dr. Phillips without leaving a trace?"

"There is no evidence of intrusion except for the theft and the attack on Dr. Phillips," Emery said. "All I can say right now is you could almost make me believe we have a ghost."

Avano's mouth tightened. "What we have here is a damned inexcusable compromise in security."

A vein in Emery's neck popped. "Every reasonable step has been taken, reviewed and retaken to protect the collections of this museum."

"How could someone have gotten into the museum, not set off the alarms and escaped with the stones without security access?" Riley asked.

Emery shook his head. "I wish I could tell you. But right now, I don't know."

"The El Zarpa stones and Dr. Phillips' research are the only items missing," Riley pointed out. "Who would want them?"

Even now, he felt something in his mind pulling

him to the stones. *Why?* The part of his brain that had been enhanced by PAX led him to see visions of the purest form of evil—terrorism. Why would a plain and simple robbery, albeit under bizarre circumstances, register the same reaction?

Or was this not a simple robbery?

Avano turned his impatient gaze on Riley. "This isn't like artwork, where you might have a collector go over the edge to take something for his private enjoyment, or thieves who'd plan to sell on the black market. There's no market for artifacts such as these. The value of the stones is as of yet undetermined, and without professional, academic evaluation, such as was taking place here under Dr. Phillips, their value may never be determined. So I can't imagine who would take them—but you'd damn well better find out."

"Just how large are these stones?" Riley questioned coolly. "How easily could they be transported?"

"Small. Each one perhaps the size of your fist." Avano described the stones, their approximate weight and number. It sounded as if they'd be easily portable. There were eleven of them, weighing no more than a few ounces each, flat and unevenly shaped.

Nina's documents and hard drive were also easily stuffed into a briefcase or even a pocket.

"The stones are insured?" Riley went on.

"Yes, but only at the standard minimum. The museum can't possibly recoup our losses for Dr. Phillips' research at that level. As I stated, the stones' true value is still unknown."

Finally letting himself turn, Riley saw Nina shake her head at something the paramedic said. Her face was white, but she sat with her back straight, her slender shoulders stiff. He was struck by the keen memory of how soft her skin felt under his hands and he knew he should have left, should have assigned another officer to head the investigative team.

He didn't want to think about the damning reasons he hadn't done that. It wasn't just PAX that had kept him here. He couldn't leave, not when he sensed evil so near to Nina.

Refocusing, he realized the museum director was laying out a plan of attack for the morning that included employee lie detector tests, new background checks and searches for everyone from the museum shop cashiers and docents to the board of directors.

"The El Zarpa stones must be recovered, the research completed," Avano demanded. "When this comes out in the papers, we're going to have hell on our hands. The museum's reputation is at stake." The director looked across the room at Nina. "Dr. Phillips' reputation is at stake."

Avano's gaze softened, and it took Riley a good

thirty seconds to comprehend the twist in his gut and name it. Jealousy. The knowledge sucker punched him in the gut, and he closed his eyes briefly against the hot burst of emotion.

What the hell was wrong with him? He wasn't one of those jerks who thought if he couldn't have a woman, then no one else should have her, either. Avano and Nina probably had a lot in common, even if there was a substantial age difference. He was Nina's mentor, and it wouldn't be surprising if she'd turned to him for comfort after Riley had—

He shut down the train of thought, focused on Avano again.

"We'll need a full list of the staff, everyone who has access to keys, especially to the secure areas." Riley ticked off more requirements, training his mind on the job at hand. Avano seemed to think that he was in charge, but he had another think coming. And maybe Riley wanted to punch him out just for looking at Nina that way, but this was the only way he could express it. "The police department will be in charge of this investigation, not the museum. Any information received through your staff in regard to the theft must be channeled directly to the police. I'll be back first thing in the morning, and I'll expect every member of the museum staff to be made available."

He didn't wait for Avano's response. He turned toward Nina. The investigation into the security system and whether it had been compromised would go forward, but for now, he had a witness.

And the fact that he'd once almost let himself love her couldn't stand in the way. Nor could the feelings still coiling and snapping inside him that told him that past wasn't quite gone.

"I'm fine," he heard her say as he approached. A paramedic was packing up her medical bag from a table near Nina.

"It's possible you have a mild concussion. There's a raised contusion, but no break in the skin. I can't make you go to the hospital for X rays, though I'd recommend it."

"Thanks, but I just want to go home."

Nina gave a forced smile that looked nothing like the Nina he'd known, and Riley felt a wrenching in his chest he didn't want to name.

What had happened to that Nina, his Nina? Complications and all, his Nina had seemed happy. Of course, she was under severe pressure with the charges of fraud, but he had a sense that there was more to the dark circles under her eyes than her work.

For all their differences, he had been tuned in to Nina to an almost metaphysical degree at one time. And tonight, just being near her, he felt it all come back. They'd been together for six months. Long enough for him to know that beneath that controlled surface she showed the world even now, there was a woman who could flame like a rocket beneath a man's claim. His claim.

The sweet passion fruit scent of her filled his senses as he neared. That scent had haunted him, taunted him, for more than a year in his memory.

She turned her head and looked up at him. From this angle, he could see the slight imperfection of a scar on her jawline where she'd fallen off a jungle gym when she was seven. He knew that and too much more about her. Her eyes locked with his for a beat. His heart kicked in his chest.

"I need to ask you some questions," he said briefly. He stared down at his notepad for a long beat, avoiding her heart-stopping green eyes in hopes of breaking the untenable connection. He met her gaze again, the past tucked away behind the wall of his heart. He'd been an expert at one time at concealing that heart.

She'd broken through all those barriers. Or almost all of them.

He forced himself to view her objectively. There was a nervous air about her, but that was to be expected under the circumstances. Or did she feel the heat still radiating between them, too?

She moved her hands, rubbed her upper arms where her short-sleeved blouse left them bare. "I'm cold," she said softly.

"Tell me what you saw," Riley said. Cool, impersonal, how he had to be. “Someone came into the storage room after you, knocked you out. What did you see?”

“Not much. I heard something, but I was already halfway down the aisle. There.” She pointed toward one of the towering shelved rows. “I looked back, but I didn’t see anything more than a shadow of movement.”

“Man or woman? Height? Weight? Anything you can tell me would help.”

She just shook her head. “The lights went out so quickly, and then all I knew was this crashing pain, and nothing. I woke up and called—” She broke off.

Him. She’d called him. He still didn’t know why, and he wasn’t prepared to ask the question.

Or maybe he wasn’t prepared for the answer.

She didn’t offer further information.

“Was the door shut, locked, after you came in?” The security chief had already outlined the procedure for entering collections storage rooms to Riley, but he wanted to hear what Nina would say.

“The lock is digital, coded. I entered the code and shut the door behind me.”

“You’re sure of that.”

“I’m sure.” She lifted her chin, tipping her face into the fluorescent light. Her skin was flawless but for the small scars above one brow and on her chin. She’d fallen during a dig in her college days, she’d told him. She was tough despite her fragile appearance, and more determined than anyone he'd ever met.

"What would you say if I told you there was no evidence of the storage room door being forced?"

She blinked. "I don't know what I would say." She looked confused. "I don't know how they could have gotten in—unless they had the code. How did they enter the museum? There must be something on the security tapes—"

"There is no evidence of a break-in. In fact, there's no evidence anyone was ever here at all."

"But I was attacked. The stones are gone."

She looked surprised now, even frightened.

"When was the last time you saw the stones, the documents, used your computer in your office?"

"I was here all day. I worked on my computer. I didn't go through the hard copies of my files today, but they were there earlier this week. I also worked in the storage room this morning, so I know the stones were here."

"What were you doing here tonight? It's late, past your normal working hours, I'm sure," he said.

She shifted and drew her arms more tightly around herself. "I often work late. I went home around five, but I usually come back in the evenings. These *are* my normal working hours."

He almost asked her why, but stopped himself.

Nina prided herself on her dedication to her work. She had an exemplary résumé and had risen quickly in the anthropological world. If she'd worked harder in the past year because she was missing something in her personal life, he didn't want to go there.

For all he knew, she could be involved in a new romantic relationship. Maybe with Avano. And he didn't want to go there, either.

"Who else works with the El Zarpa stones?"

Nina furrowed her brow. "There's Juliet Manet, my assistant. But she primarily works with my documentation and data. It's my project. I'm the only one who works directly with the stones. They're too valuable—"

"But the director just told me they have no established value."

"Not yet." There was a new strain in her voice. "We have to get them back. We just have to."

Riley wished he could tell her the stones would be recovered, but he couldn't. He couldn't put his arms around her, either, and he damned himself for wanting to. He hoped to God this was about the stones, not about Nina. And even more, he hoped his senses were wrong, that something evil wasn't this close to Nina.

"What about your files? Do you have backups of what was taken from your office?"

She nodded. "At home."

"You'll want to put them in a safe place now," he pointed out. "And you'll need to make them available to the investigation in case there's anything we can glean that will lead us to what the thieves were after in selecting them."

Nina suddenly pressed a hand to her forehead. "Are we done?"

"No." At the look of exhaustion on her face, Riley flipped his notebook shut. "But it's after eleven. The rest of my questions can wait. Go home."

He needed to wait. He needed time to assimilate all the conflicting sensations coming at him. Time to deal with the dull roar of blood rushing through his veins whenever he came near her.

There was no going back, though. He knew that. Nina had needed something he would never be and had been a fool even to have attempted to be. A man who could fit into her high-society, intellectual world, a man who could create a family and a future with her in that world. For that, she'd have to find another man. Riley didn't even fit into his own world anymore.

He'd made his decision that final day in the hospital when she'd come to see him. He'd been gone three months in a remote PAX clinic before being returned to a D.C. rehabilitation hospital for his reentry into normal life—or what passed for normal for him now. Nina had come to see him, and he'd sent her away. It had been the right decision, no matter how many times he'd regretted it. As much as he'd never fit into her world at one time, she'd never fit into his now. His world carried a high calling, but it was accompanied by a high price. He had no right to ask Nina to pay it.

Then Nina stuck her hand in her purse and gasped.

"My keys," she said suddenly and looked up at him, her eyes wide. "They're gone."

Chapter 3

She could have said no. She could have come up with a thousand—a million—reasons to say no. She could have requested that another officer escort her home.

But there she was, snapping her seat belt secure in Riley's unmarked police car. The lights and sounds of the city blurred past her eyes as he drove.

He'd accompanied her back to her burgled office, and she'd double-checked that she hadn't left her keys there. By the time Nina had put on her sweater and followed Riley to his car, she was almost too exhausted to be unnerved anymore. Nothing seemed real.

"You can't go home alone," Riley had said at first. "Not if someone has your keys."

"Maybe I just misplaced them," she'd told him. "You don't know that someone took them." She was confused; for all she knew, she'd locked them inside her car before she'd gone into the museum. She hadn't thought of that possibility until they'd already left the institute. "I want to go home." They'd stolen her stones, stolen her research. What would anyone want from her apartment?

"Then you're not going there alone," he'd said grimly.

He had been so insistent that she had known argument was pointless. Or maybe that just had been her excuse. It felt almost dreamlike, riding in Riley's car. The scent of him slid around her, warm as her sweater, dangerous as the night.

Being with him this way was all too starkly familiar, she thought as she slid a sideways glance at his forbidding profile. A five o'clock shadow darkened his jaw, lending an even more dangerous look to him. He pulled her, though, always had, with that fascinating, no-holds-barred air he had. In the safe world she'd always lived in, he was a walk on the wild side, and she'd taken that walk willingly. That it had ended badly shouldn't have surprised her, but somehow it had. There was a reason she'd followed the rules all her life.

She'd met him at a charity function and had thrown all the rules out the window. He'd been seated next to her at the banquet and he'd been as bored as her. He'd been there representing the police department, and she'd been there representing a big fat check from her father. She was on the charity's board and she'd been in touch with him a few times on the phone; she had already been half in love with his deep, roughly sexy Texas voice. She'd made an impulsive joke. *Let's sneak out the back.*

He'd taken a dark, piercing look at her and called her bluff. The chicken was rubbery, the speeches never-ending, and the man next to her dangerously attractive. They'd driven out into the seductive night, in this very car. He'd bought her a drink in a bar and then taken her back to her car, kissing her in a sizzling, once-in-a-lifetime kind of way, and said goodbye. She'd lost her mind and her heart in one fell swoop. Maybe she wouldn't have ever seen him again but two days later, she'd fallen down an icy set of steps and been knocked out on the street.

Waiting for an ambulance, passersby had used her cell phone to try to contact someone who knew her. When no one had answered, they'd gone through her call log. They'd called Riley, and he'd come to the scene. He'd ridden with her to the hospital, and he'd driven her back home. The man who'd been little more than her sexy stranger, her one-time kiss in the night, had been amazingly gentle and sweet. And somehow, something that might otherwise never have happened had begun.

Nina cut the painful memories off with brutal precision. The humiliation of the past was too excruciating to replay with Riley a mere two feet away. *He'd* been hurt. *He'd* been in the hospital. And *he'd* wanted nothing to do with her.

He parked in front of the building where she had an apartment on the tenth floor.

"I'm sorry," he said. At first, she wasn't sure what he was apologizing for—she was thrown back to the day he'd sent her away, and she actually thought—

"The loss of the stones must be a huge blow."

Of course. He was talking about the robbery. "I can't believe this is happening." Maybe she was in some kind of denial. She was going to wake up tomorrow and this was all going to have been a nightmare.

"Has there been any unusual interest in the stones?" he asked then. "I mean, beyond the media and the El Zarpan government."

Her chest tightened. He knew about the accusations of fraud, of course. Who didn't? It was all over the news.

"I don't know what you mean by unusual interest," she said tensely. "The only people with a real stake in the stones are anthropologists and archaeologists. The El Zarpa stones are an incredible find and could change how we look at history."

"Do you think the stones are real?" he asked point-blank, his face expressionless. What did he think of her now? Did he believe the news reports, the rumors, the embarrassing charges?

Nina's spine stiffened. "I didn't participate in any fraud, if that's what you're getting at." She didn't want to care what he thought of her but, dammit, she did.

He shook his head. "That's not what I mean." The stern flatness of his voice gentled slightly. "Who carved these stones? Where did they get their sophisticated knowledge?"

"That's the sixty-four-thousand-dollar question." She bit her lip, stared out the windshield at the sluicing rain. "I think they're real." She looked back at him. "Or maybe I just want to think they're real. I'm positive they're quite old. As for the knowledge, legend has it the knowledge came from ancient astronauts who left Earth thousands of years ago. Ancient spacemen, if you will, who had supernatural powers from beyond our universe. Supposedly, dark shamans possessed the stones for thousands of years. Then the stones were hidden away to prevent man from using them for evil purposes."

Riley listened, his dark eyes hard on hers in the shadowed car. She was struggling for control. She needed to be alone, where she could scream. Maybe even cry.

"Evil purposes?" he prompted.

She pinned her gaze on the clock in the dash, concentrating on the digital numbers, watching them roll over as a beat passed while she pulled herself together. Somehow, she managed to answer his question in mechanical fashion.

"Shamans accessed the spirit world, controlled everything from the tides to the crops. Their powers could be used for evil, as well. The highest shamans claimed their power came from the stones. It's a fascinating study in the cultural anthropology of superstition, but of course that doesn't explain the sophisticated knowledge exhibited in the El Zarpa stones."

"What explains that?"

Something she didn't want to define banded her chest as she lifted her eyes to him again. "I don't know." She knew she hadn't perpetrated a hoax, but what if a hoax had been perpetrated on her? The El Zarpa stones were impractical, unscientific, out of this world. The secret side of her researcher's heart had wanted to believe in magic, just once.

But maybe all she'd been was a fool.

Riley watched her for a long while through the dark. The last remnants of the rainstorm tapped on the top of the car. Even from two feet away, she could smell him, that musky, complicated scent that made hormones leap and jerk inside her, and she knew there'd been more than one time in her life when she'd believed in magic. But that hadn't worked out, either.

"Can you think of anyone who might have a grudge against you, wish you harm? Or even wish your father harm?"

Nina blinked. "I hadn't thought of that," she said.

"Your father is a powerful political figure. His daughter's charged with fraud. It's an embarrassment."

"That's a stretch," she pointed out. "I'm a full-grown adult. My father has no influence or dealings with the institute. You don't— You don't really think this has anything to do with my father, do you?"

He was silent for a beat. "Probably not. But we can't ignore any possibility. What about anyone holding a grudge?"

She shook her head vigorously. "I don't have enemies." A shiver tingled down her spine in spite of her strong denial. "That I know of," she added.

"What about friends?" he asked then. "Relationships? Who are you close to, Nina? Who knows your habits, your routine?"

"Juliet works with me, or with my data, as I mentioned before. Dr. Avano is the director of the museum and oversees my research. There are all sorts of research assistants, fellow scientists, at the museum, but over the past year, I can't say I've been terribly friendly with any of them," she admitted. "I've been pretty much consumed with the stones." Sudden emotion pricked her eyes. God, she was tired. She looked away. "I have to get them back."

The rain patted down for a painful moment as the horror of the evening pressed down on her again. Then Riley said, "Come on. Let's go up."

The doorman let them in and provided a spare key to the apartment. The embossed carpeting and gleaming brass fixtures of the sleek lobby only served to remind Nina that her money had always been a source of tension between herself and Riley. She didn't earn a huge living, despite the years that had gone into her Ph.D. in anthropology. But thanks to her family, she had a solid investment portfolio that afforded her a home in a downtown building close to the museum. She didn't indulge in many luxuries, but her apartment was one of them.

Riley rarely spoke of his background, but she knew he'd grown up in a boys' home, an orphanage. He didn't have family or family money. She didn't care. There'd been a time when she would have gladly ditched her whole life for a shack in the woods with Riley.

Damn him for not wanting her enough to abandon his pride and let her do it.

We're too different. That had been the only explanation he'd given her that final day. The accident had caused him to reevaluate his life, set new priorities. She hadn't made the cut.

The thought made her stop as they entered the elevator. She put her hand on the door to hold it open.

"I'm sure I'll be fine," she said. "You don't need to come up. I can get Franz to come with me, check the apartment." She nodded toward the doorman. "I'm sure he wouldn't mind."

"Does Franz have a gun?" Riley entered the elevator, punched the button for the third floor. "I didn't think so."

Nina let the door close. He was right. She should have insisted that a different officer escort her home. One who hadn't broken her heart.

The elevator took them smoothly to the third floor. Nina didn't let herself look at Riley as she walked out into the corridor. She was so close to the edge, and she knew it. Tomorrow, maybe she'd be stronger.

She tried not to think about having had thirteen months to deal with the loss of Riley and not doing one iota better than she had the day she'd walked out of the rehabilitation hospital. Enclosed in the intimacy of the elevator with him, her knees had trembled. She had felt him watching her. She should be long over him, and she wasn't anywhere close.

The short walk down the corridor seemed to take forever.

"Wait here," he said when they reached her apartment. Taking the key the doorman had given her, he put it into the lock, then stopped cold.

She felt cold watching him, and she shivered as he withdrew the key and lifted dead eyes to her. She reached for the door.

"Wait." He grabbed her arm.

"Why?" Nina stood firm. What was wrong with him? His eyes were scaring her.

"Something's wrong here." He pulled her. "Don't ask questions right now. Just come with me."

God, was he insane? She didn't know what was going on. Riley had not been the same since that crash. The doctors had tried to tell her that sometimes people were *never* the same after a head injury, that it wasn't unusual for relationships—even marriages—to fall apart after that kind of trauma.

The night of the accident was a horrible blur in her memory. Fellow police officers had been there, but she hadn't known any of them. He'd never introduced her to any of his friends on the force. She'd haunted the hospital for days while he'd lain in critical condition, comatose. They wouldn't let her see him.

Then he'd quite simply vanished from the hospital. Taken to a specialized clinic for newly developed, experimental surgery, she'd been told. They wouldn't tell her where the clinic was. They wouldn't tell her anything. She wasn't family. As far as they were concerned, she was no one. Riley had no family, she'd tearfully pleaded, but in vain.

She'd gone to the police station, but they wouldn't tell her anything, either, no matter how many times she called and came by. She wouldn't have even known when he had come back to D.C., to the rehabilitation hospital, if one of the officers at the department hadn't finally taken pity on her and let her know that he was there. She'd rushed to the hospital.

The Riley she'd found there was not the Riley she'd remembered, the Riley she'd grieved for over the three months he'd been gone. His abrupt dismissal had been like the lash of a whip, sharp and burning, on her heart. To her credit, she'd neither begged nor cried, not in front of him at least. There had been no doubt about the strength of his conviction. His voice had been so final, his eyes so dead, when he'd told her to go away.

Dead like they were now.

Chapter 4

In the shadow world of the dark sight, Riley saw stones etched with symbols. Saw a dark figure placing them in some kind of order—but he couldn't see the pattern. The sight veered through a misty vortex, swayed, then was sucked backward through space and time.

And all he could hear was Nina screaming.

Riley snapped back into his body.

"This is my home." Nina pulled her arm from his hold, snatched the key out of his hand, pivoted quickly, shoved the key into the lock, threw open the door and reached for the light switch. Then the scream wasn't in his vision; the scream was here, real. Nina.

The low lamplight streaming through from the living room revealed the disastrous state of her apartment. Cushions and pillows were strewn from the couch. Drawers were pulled out, knickknacks dumped everywhere. Her home had been thoroughly ransacked. Riley's heart practically stopped beating as he reached for Nina's shaking body. His gaze shot around, probing, seeking.

"Oh my God," she breathed.

Riley let go of her. "Don't move. You don't know if they're gone."

He couldn't stand the thought of what could have happened to Nina if she'd come home alone. The prickling sense of evil that had lurked in the museum came at him harder here now.

The sudden thick silence of the building weighed heavily. He wanted her out of here, now. He wanted her somewhere safe.

A new tide of energy rolled over him. *Fire. Vicious leaping waves of lava swallowing everything in their path. Screams of burning people roared in his ears. Hands reached, disappeared, from the thick liquid heat.*

The air rushed back around him and Riley staggered, regained his balance. The vision swirled at the edges of his consciousness, urgent.

Nina's frightened gaze held him. "What's happening?" she whispered starkly.

"I want you to get back in the elevator and go downstairs. Get Franz to call the police. Stay with him." He forced himself to take another step from her, to detach himself from her.

From the hallway, he heard voices. The strained faces of a balding man in a silk dressing gown and a middle-aged woman in curlers and cold cream peeked into the apartment.

"What about you?" Nina asked, placing her hand on his arm as he moved away. He had no choice but to turn back.

Her eyes were a clear bottle-green, fragile as glass. But he had to hand it to her, she'd recovered, gotten herself back under control. She was tight and tense, though. He knew she was scared to death, even if she didn't want him to know it.

"If someone's here, I'm not letting them get away," he told her.

"What's going on?" the man in the robe asked. "I heard a scream." His look was a cross between morbid curiosity and irritation. It was an expensive apartment building, and his expensive sleep had been disturbed.

Riley reached into his hip pocket and flashed his badge. "The scene isn't secured. I recommend for your own safety you wait inside your apartments. I'll be with you shortly to take your statements in case you've seen or heard anything. Nina—"

"I'm okay here." Heels dug in, she wasn't moving. Her hands were balled fists at her sides now. "You have no backup. What if—"

"You're not my backup, Nina."

Something painful flashed briefly in her expression. Guilt slammed into him like a rogue wave. He didn't want to do or say anything to hurt Nina. But the thought of her doing anything to put herself in danger made him nauseous. He was a trained professional; she was not.

The neighbors weren't moving. In fact, the woman with the curlers craned her neck to get a better view of the apartment.

"Oh, my, look at your apartment!" she gasped.

Nina didn't need the reminder. Riley watched her fighting the emotion she seemed determined to keep in check. But she wasn't looking for sympathy from him or her neighbors. Unless something had changed, she didn't know her neighbors well. Nina kept to herself, had few close friends and, as far as he'd ever seen, she wasn't very close to her family. Senator Jackson Phillips wasn't exactly Mr. Warm and Cuddly, and Daria Phillips was one of the most self-absorbed women he'd ever met.

Not that her parents had liked him much, either. It had been a mutual distaste society every time Nina had brought him around them. Her parents rued the day he and Nina had ever met. And they were right.

He and Nina weren't meant to be together. She'd been looking for excitement, and he'd been there. But in the end, he'd known she'd be looking for a husband and a picket fence, all tied up in a neat bow in a house in Georgetown.

It was his own damn fault things had gone as far as they had. It had taken him all this time to get her out of his system, yet here he stood, feeling things he didn't want to feel, remembering things he didn't want to remember.

It had been ridiculous for them to be together. They'd complemented each other, for a while. He was simple, she was anything but. They'd challenged each other. She'd made him try opera and caviar, and he'd taken her out to a farm belonging to the family of another officer and dared her to get on a horse with him.

And mostly they'd made love like two teenagers, urgent and hungry and heedless.

He reached for the cell phone clipped to his belt and pretended he couldn't still feel the soft glide of her sweat-slicked skin in his mind. "I need backup." He gave Nina's address, punched off and gave her a stern look. "Don't move from this spot."

He checked out the front door, but could see no signs of tampering. Nina's keys had been taken from the museum, but it still added up to another break-in with no sign of forced entry. Two break-ins in one evening with no forced entry. He didn't like what that was adding up to in light of the fraud. He didn't like what he knew his superiors at the police department were going to think. The museum theft had all the earmarks of an inside job.

And the link between the two of them was Nina. She'd been accused of fraud, and now the stones in question had disappeared. Getting rid of the stones could look like a desperate move to hide her alleged crime.

But if Nina's stones were connected to the kind of evil he was programmed to pick up, she was in a hell of a lot more trouble than that. She could be right in the middle of something extremely dangerous.

The ancients believed the stones held power. Superstition, Nina had called it. Were his visions keying in to a primeval past or a catastrophic future?

Or was it his own past with Nina that was sending his senses out of control? He was still a living, breathing lab rat, with too little experience with his new abilities to draw on.

He flipped the light on in the kitchen. The collection of sea glass she'd kept on a shelf above the sink lay in broken pieces on the floor, as if swept there angrily. Pottery and silverware lay everywhere, drawers were pulled out. From there, he moved on to the short corridor leading to the two bedrooms. He knew Nina used one as an office; the other was her bedroom.

Adrenaline pumping and gripping his gun, he tapped the door open to the office. No sound. He stepped into the room, wheeled, pulled open the closet door. Nothing. Just boxes overturned, their contents spewed, and out-of-season clothes hanging on a rack. He spun back around to take in the desk area. The hard drive to her computer was missing, and he felt a buzz at the edges of his consciousness, the same buzz he'd felt when he'd entered the apartment.

He closed his eyes, opened his mind to the vision.

Earth ruptured, torn apart, breaking into chasms of never-ending black depths. The ground vibrated beneath his feet, ripping open again and again.

Riley's eyes flashed open. His skin tingled, burned, and he popped back into his body. Again, the sense of urgency drummed in his veins. He was seeing large-scale disasters of varying types. But these weren't terror attacks. They were natural disasters. He could make no sense of the images.

The bedroom was empty of intruders, as well. The mattress had been shoved aside, searched as if someone thought she could be hiding something beneath it. The aristocratic elegance of her French-style suite made the shambles it was now more striking. *You'd think a princess slept here,* he'd told her once, with the gilded coronet over the bed hung with cascading silk drapes.

A princess does sleep here, Nina had quipped back. Then she'd stripped out of her satin teddy and whispered a few royal commands that had made him forget all about his discomfort with her decor.

She'd been good at that—making him forget that not so much as his little pinkie toe fit in her world. But the reminders were everywhere, and even if the accident hadn't happened, they never would have made it.

Or that's what he had to believe, because anything else would make him crazy.

The wisp of satin material peeking out from beneath an overturned drawer could make him crazy, too. Nina's private things lay all over the floor. Private things he'd seen her wear. Private things he'd taken off her with his teeth.

He tore his gaze off the intimate objects and forced his mind to the task at hand. This was his job, and unfortunately Nina was smack in the middle of it, for some reason.

He'd deal with it like a professional, even if it killed him. Somehow, he had to put some distance between himself and the all-too-personal aspects of the case. If he let emotions send his powers offtrack, a lot of lives could be in danger. He was as keenly aware of that as PAX was. They'd made him what he was, but he had yet to prove himself, to prove that what they'd planted in his brain could do what they intended.

He wanted to prove himself. No matter that he hadn't asked for this job, he wanted it now, deeply. The possibility that he could save countless lives with his abilities filled the deep, aching hole that had been his life. He'd been searching for some kind of meaning when he'd joined the police force, and had found it in a job he did well and through the opportunity to help people who were helpless, the way he'd been once. The scale of that meaning was that much greater in his work for PAX.

He moved quickly back to the front of the apartment. The little group of neighbors had swelled and now included a uniformed security officer from the apartment building. Riley briefed him on the situation, then turned back to Nina.

The shell shock in her eyes told him she hadn't fully taken in what had happened. She'd already had more than enough tonight after the attack at the museum. She was holding up, but he knew that was a facade.

"The apartment's clear," he told her. "There's no one here." He saw no relief in her tense face.

"I don't understand," she said softly, thickly, low for his ears alone. "What's happening?"

Her life was falling apart, that's what was happening. He wanted to reach out, pull her into his arms, give her some kind of comfort. No way could he trust himself to do that.

And now he had to give her more bad news.

"What do you keep at home in connection to the El Zarpa stones?" he asked. "Your hard drive is missing. You mentioned backups from the museum. Anything else?"

She blinked. "Just the backups of my research on the hard drives. I keep my most recent work on disk because I switch back and forth between the office and home. The disk I worked on this evening was here when I went back to the museum. Are my disks gone?" Panic entered her voice. "I came home earlier in the evening. I brought the disk with me, but I had an idea I wanted to check out. I wanted to look at one of the stones again, so I went back to the institute and—"

"I can't tell what else is missing."

She moved purposefully past him, and he took hold of her arm. "I have to see." She tried to shake his grip.

"You can't touch anything. Not until the scene's cleared."

"I have to see!"

He could see that desperate front she was working so hard to keep up cracking at the edges. But still she was so fierce. Her research meant everything to her. He knew that better than anyone. He'd never known anyone more driven than Nina. She held herself to the highest of standards, which is why he couldn't imagine her involved with anything fraudulent. There wasn't anything in her life that wasn't perfect.

Except, for a short time, him.

"We'll see together," he relented, "but don't touch anything."

He walked her down the hall to the office. He'd left the door open, and he waited while she went inside. He had no doubt her desk had been neat as a pin when she'd left it. There wasn't a slobby bone in Nina's body, not when it came to her work. Despair dragged on her shoulders as he watched her take in the shambles of her once pristine workspace.

"I don't see any of my disks," she said dully.

"You can look more thoroughly later, after we've cleared the crime scene," he told her, and he saw her flinch at having her apartment described as a crime scene. This was her home, her haven. It was her life, not just her workspace, that had been invaded.

The zap of something ever-present at the boundaries of his mind shot to the surface. The sight took him quickly, familiar now. *A hand aligning the stones. Then a shadow, Nina's face—*

He tumbled back into his body. He reached for the doorjamb to keep his balance. The energy burned on in his veins.

"I didn't see any sign of forced entry," he said.

"Are you sure your apartment was locked when you left?" It had been locked when they'd arrived.

"Yes." She looked away, her expression stiff.

Nina wasn't the type to break down in front of other people. She didn't get angry or upset. In the six months they'd been together, he'd never seen her cry, not even that last day at the hospital.

He sensed imminent danger, and whether it was emotion affecting his senses or not, he wasn't running any risks. But he knew, too, that there was no way for him to adequately explain that to her. Knowing a little about PAX was like being a little bit pregnant.

His instincts tugged him back to the remote vision of the stones' alignment.

"How are the engravings in the stones connected?" he asked. "Are they ordered in some way?"

Nina gave him a baffled look.

"The stones are all different. They carry a common theme of advanced technology and understanding of the earth, and there is a figure in each of the stones, but no, they aren't ordered in any particular way."

"What did your research into the stones entail? What was on the missing disks?"

"Digital images, notes, research files. We hadn't allowed any outside photography. We did allow selected experts and some members of the media to view them when I first brought them back. But my work on the stones had just begun and we weren't ready to go fully public, put them on display, until we could authenticate their origin. I was against taking the story to the media at all, but the institute board ruled against me."

"Tremaine."

Riley glanced over his shoulder. The other officers had arrived.

"Wait here," he told Nina. "I've got to talk to them, and I'm going to take statements from your neighbors."

Nina stared after Riley. Where did he think she was going to go? She had a ball of panic in her stomach, and her head pounded. Her stones had been stolen, and her apartment had been ransacked.

And she felt guilty. She'd lied, if only by omission. In a fit of paranoia the week before, she'd stashed a copy of her research on a disk in the locked glove box of her car. With the fraud allegations, she'd been frightened the institute would hand the stones back over to the El Zarpan government, perhaps even seize her research. She should have told Riley, but he'd already told her the police wanted to review her research. That one disk was all she had left.

She'd make another copy, then give it to Riley tomorrow. That would have to be good enough. For now, she wasn't telling anyone about it—not when every known copy of her research had disappeared.

But why? Her research into the stones would have been published eventually, and certainly whoever stole them could never publish any findings without revealing his identity. Who would want her research and the stones so desperately that he'd break into her apartment to steal something he could never reveal? There *were* people who stole artwork for underground private collections—but who would even want stones everyone thought were fakes?

Unless someone else thought the stones were real...

But still, why?

"Nina?"

She jumped at Riley's voice.

"I know you're tired," he said, concern in his voice.

Stupidly, she wanted to cling to that concern, cling to him. She was aware of her heart beating too fast; it hurt just to look at him.

She was still attracted to him, and that was understandable. It was a physical, biological reaction, and she was in a vulnerable situation. It was natural for her to feel needy. But it made no sense that she still hurt so much. Riley wasn't hurting. She wasn't sure he'd ever really cared deeply enough about her to be hurt by their breakup. He'd cut her out of his life without a qualm.

"I need you to do a thorough walk-through," he went on. "Tell me if you see anything else missing."

She nodded. "Okay."

There was an officer at the door, dusting it with a fine charcoal powder. Great. More mess. Riley walked her through the living room. She had to step over tossed throw pillows. Standing in the middle of the room, she felt a wave of violation and for the first time, anger poked through the fear.

"These are pretty valuable, aren't they?" Riley nodded toward a pair of *chicha* jars that had been knocked onto the Aubusson carpet from a walnut sidetable.

She nodded mutely. Her collection of pre-Columbian art was not made up of actual ancient items—those belonged in a museum—but the items she had in her home were gallery quality. That nothing valuable was missing—nothing but her research—just made her feel sicker.

It was the same scene in every room—she couldn't see anything missing. They took prints from the desk area and in her bedroom from the drawers that held her jewelry. When she was allowed to open them, everything was there, down to the sapphire earrings Riley had given her only a few weeks before his crash.

When they walked back out to the living room, the officers were packing up their kits. Riley closed the door behind him, shutting out the straggling remainder of curious neighbors.

Her apartment had seemed empty and huge only hours earlier when she'd been here alone. Now Riley stood there, filling her entry hall, and it shrank. His dark brown hair was still damp from their dash inside in the rain. The jacket he wore was unzipped, revealing the chambray shirt tucked into belted jeans snug against his muscular thighs. She could just see the gun strapped across his shoulder, disappearing beneath his jacket.

He watched her with those enigmatic eyes of his. His eyes frightened her, especially in the odd moments when they seemed to go dead. Then they would come alive again and they would make her feel ridiculously safe.

"Did anyone see anything?" she asked, remembering he'd taken statements.

He shook his head. "No, but sometimes people think of something later. Franz doesn't remember letting in anyone suspicious, but they'll check the tapes. They've got surveillance cameras in the lobby and outside the building."

She nodded. The building was highly secure. Fat lot of good that had done her. The museum was secure, too.

"We need to talk about the stones," he said. "But not tonight. You've been through enough today."

The low, lazy slide of his cowboy voice sounded casual, but his mind was sharper than any she'd ever known. "Are you going to grill me?" she asked. She'd meant the remark to be off-the-cuff, but then she picked up on something awkward in his eyes that set off a ping of dread in her stomach. "I know there was no evidence of a break-in at the museum." She remembered his earlier questions at the institute. *Was she sure she'd locked the door behind her? Why was she working late? What would she say if he told her there was no sign of forced entry?*

A few weeks ago, she wouldn't have believed anyone would suspect her of anything. She lived by the rules, did everything right. She'd never even had a parking ticket. She'd gotten straight A's in school and earned good citizenship awards. She thanked people, said please and ate her vegetables.

"You think I took the stones from the museum myself. I ransacked my apartment and pretended to lose my keys, and now the disks with my research are gone, both here and at the museum. It all fits. Oh my God." She'd been accused of fraud, and now it would look as if she'd gotten rid of all the evidence. Hiding a disk would hardly make her look more innocent.

She backed away from Riley's dark stare, horrified. What had become of her life?

"Nina—" He came toward her.

She bumped up against the doorjamb to the kitchen. She wanted to run, from Riley, from her life. But where would she go? "You think I did all of this!"

Chapter 5

"No, I don't think that." Riley grabbed her by the shoulders and gently shook her. "Listen to me. Asking questions is my job. That doesn't mean I think you're guilty. If you're innocent, a thorough investigation should clear your name."

"*If* I'm innocent?"

She couldn't stand his look of pity, nor did the promise of an investigation make her feel better. Things looked bad, no matter what he said. And if she never got the stones back…

"Let go of me." She wrestled away from his hold, heat and frustration tangling inside her. "Either arrest me or leave me alone!"

"Dammit, Nina, no one's talking about arresting you. But you can't stay here. Someone has your keys."

"If someone really took my keys, really ransacked my apartment, don't you mean?"

"That's not what I mean at all." His gaze remained hard and unrelenting. "It'd be outright stupidity to stay here until you have your locks changed when a set of your keys is out there. And I must believe your keys were stolen or I wouldn't want you to leave."

He stepped toward her, closing the gap she'd tried to create, taking away her buffer, and suddenly she was frightened he was going to offer her some kind of comfort, but that was crazy. Her heart hammered—not in fear, she realized with a shock—but with anticipation. She went from hot to shivery in the space of a beat. If she swayed toward him... If their lips met... *What was she thinking?* He wasn't going to touch her, much less kiss her.

She was tired and having idiotic thoughts. She'd like nothing better than for Riley to put his arms around her right now and lie to her that everything was going to be okay. He could lie to her about a lot of things and she'd like it.

That was scary.

"I know you didn't do this, Nina," he said, his stern face gentling. "I know you're innocent. It's going to be all right."

She closed her eyes against the tenderness of his reassurance. "You don't know that."

"Nina…"

She needed a minute, just a minute, to pull herself together. No way was she unraveling in front of Riley.

A warm hand touched her shoulder, pulled her toward him. Then her face was buried in his hard chest. He tightened his arms around her, running his hands over her shoulders and back. Oh God, this was wrong on so many levels.

"I'm okay," she whispered thickly, lifting her head.

"You don't look okay," he said.

She had to tip her chin to meet his eyes, but with his face lowered toward hers, they were nose to nose. Worse, mouth to mouth. If he so much as moved… Or if she…

"Nina," he said, and there was suddenly something soul-stirring in the husky depth of his voice.

For an interminable moment, neither of them moved. She was keenly aware of his arms still around her, of his heat pressing against hers, even more aware of the hard ridge of him against her body. The electric memory of passion crackled between them.

Her senses flickered and she knew, just knew, that if he lowered his head another inch—

How could she have ever thought his eyes were dead? They looked hellishly alive now, desperate somehow. As desperate as she was. He still desired her. He hadn't ever loved her, but he wanted her.

Potential disaster lay a heartbeat, a breath, away. She knew without hesitation that she wanted him as much as she had ever wanted him, in every way imaginable. If she ripped her clothes off, maybe she could even talk him into a night of auld lang syne. But great sex with Riley was just that. Great sex. And she had enough problems in her life without courting more.

She found the strength to pull away from him, putting distance between herself and the danger of her emotions. Her knees felt rubbery and she could feel the rapid-fire beat of her pulse and the scorch of *him,* no matter how far she moved away.

"Tell me where I can take you tonight," he said then. She turned, and their gazes held across the space she'd put between them.

Her head throbbed. He was right. She couldn't stay here. "I'll call my parents," she lied. Her parents were in Europe, some kind of international trade powwow.

He watched her for a long beat. He shouldn't have looked safe to her. He wasn't safe at all. He was dangerous, as the gun he wore reminded her. He might be a man of the law, but he'd broken her heart. She needed him to leave.

"Call them now," he said.

"I don't need supervision."

He strode past her, yanked the portable phone off the base and came back, pushing it into her hand.

"Call them or I'll call them for you."

He would, dammit. She pushed buttons and pretended to speak to her father. She moved the phone away from her mouth. "He'll be right over to pick me up. You can go." As soon as Riley left, she could call a cab. She'd take the spare key she had to her parents' house and get out of her ruined apartment.

If only she could escape her ruined life as easily.

Before she could react, Riley reached out and took the phone, held it to his ear.

"This is the time and temperature reading, Nina."

He slammed the phone down on the entry table.

"My parents are in Europe," she said, frustration choking her voice. "But I've got a set of keys for their house. Don't worry—there wasn't a copy of their key on the key ring I lost. I'll get a cab and go straight there, I promise. I'm not going to stay here tonight. Are you satisfied now? You're free to go."

"No. I'm not satisfied at all. Even five minutes is too long for you to stay here alone when the apartment can't be secured."

The implication of his words sent a shiver up her spine. What did he know that she didn't know?

She remembered the way he'd tried to stop her from entering her apartment.

"How did you know that something was wrong in my apartment?" she breathed starkly. "You knew! You told me not to go in."

He was silent for a taut beat and she saw a darkness hollow his eyes, turning them from blue to almost pure black. The hairs on the nape of her neck tingled.

"You'd just been attacked at the museum," he said. "Your office had been burgled, the stones stolen. Your keys had disappeared."

His answer didn't satisfy her. She felt confused and uncertain of everything, especially Riley. The more time she spent with him tonight, the more she realized he was different in some indefinable way. A certain mystery cloaked his eyes that had never been there before. An energy came off him in waves. Or was that energy coming from her, from the awareness she couldn't deny, even now when so much stood between them?

The brain injury had changed him, she knew that. She'd had sympathetic, pitying doctors explain it to her.

But their explanations didn't explain what she was feeling now. Maybe she'd just been too long without any real human connection. She didn't need anyone, or so she'd tried to convince herself, but it wasn't true. She needed Riley, had needed him for thirteen lonely months.

The silence stretched. Outside, wind beat against the windows.

Whatever is happening, you're in the middle of it.

"I have no intention of spending the night here," she said, her voice shaking despite her best efforts. "But I'll be fine till the cab comes. I'll even wait downstairs with Franz. I don't understand—"

He was too near again and she ached for his hot touch once more.

"You don't need a cab. I'm here. Let me drive you over there, for my own peace of mind if nothing else."

His gaze was solemn, but she could see that edge of need still lurking. Her heart beat panicked wings against the wall of her chest. Somehow, she had to end this torment of his nearness; if letting him drive her to Falls Church was what it took, then he was giving her no choice.

She hated being scared. And she hated that it was Riley who made her feel safe.

"All right," she said finally. "Let's go."

The senator lived in a three-story Federal-style mansion in the Virginia suburb outside D.C. Riley'd been there once. Nina had invited him to join her parents at their Falls Church home for dinner on Christmas Eve.

He'd nearly choked on the name-dropping and condescension, the clear lack of welcome and the coldness. From the dizzying array of flatware to the political conversation, they had made sure he knew that he didn't fit in. As if he hadn't known that to begin with.

He stopped the car at the gate. Elaborate iron fencing bordered the expansive property. He pushed the button to lower the car's automatic window and leaned out to punch in the security code as Nina gave it to him. The place was like Fort Knox. She'd brought a small overnight bag from her apartment and she would be safe here tonight. That was all that mattered—not the memories, not the reminders.

The gates silently yawned open.

He pulled the car around the drive and got out. The rain had stopped, but the night was damp and chill. She'd opened her own door before he got there. She didn't want his help, not one single bit.

And he— He felt desperate, even out of control. He could have kissed her back there in her apartment. And if he had, he didn't know if he would have been able to stop. He'd been overwhelmed by her nearness, by the aching sensation of her body in his arms.

The heavy rise of his desire had been a physical response, but he knew far too sharply that his reaction had been more than physical. She'd ripped at his heart.

"I'll be fine now," she told him after they climbed the stone steps and reached the massive oak door. Her face remained carefully guarded.

"Have your locks changed at your apartment tomorrow," he reminded her.

The wind had died down. The sky was clearing. The moon broke through the scudding clouds. Nina's eyes looked fragile, but her jaw was determinedly independent.

"I'll take care of it," she promised. "Please don't worry about me." She juggled the overnight bag to insert the key into her parents' door. Inside, she flipped on a light that revealed the perfectly buffed floor. The entry hall was huge. Tapestries hung on the walls and even now, with her parents out of town, fresh flowers had been left on the marble-topped table. She immediately turned to punch numbers into a security box beside the door, then looked back at him.

She stood there for a moment, the candescent glow from the huge chandelier in the mansion's foyer lighting the coppery streaks in her hair.

"Thank you for bringing me here," she said finally.

"If you need a ride back to the museum in the morning to get your car..." What the hell had made him offer?

"I don't need a ride. I'll take care of it."

Riley watched the door close behind Nina. He sat in his car and watched the front hall light go out, watched an upstairs light blink on. He imagined Nina moving up the grand staircase to her old room, the one where she'd grown up. She'd taken him up there on that one occasion he'd visited the Phillips' mansion. He'd seen all her awards on the walls and the showroom neatness of her so-called child's bedroom.

To his shock, her bedroom had actually made him sentimental for a moment for the plain and simple Texas boys' ranch where he'd grown up. As bare of warmth as it had been, it had not been as cold as the senator's fine mansion.

That was when he'd realized she had empty places inside her, too, just as he did. And it had scared him to death to think that she thought he might be able to fill them.

Alone in the shadows, he punched a number on his cell phone. The prickling sensations of evil that had haunted him all night and the visions that had pounded him in Nina's apartment… He still had no idea what they added up to, but the potential couldn't be ignored.

"Tremaine here," he said.

A few minutes later, he disconnected the call.

The case was officially out of the hands of the D.C. police department, whether they knew it or not.

Chapter 6

She was shocked that she had slept at all.

The last thing Nina had thought before she had fallen asleep was that her stones were gone. And it was the first thing on her mind when she woke.

She'd first become fascinated with pre-Columbian antiquities when she'd traveled to Peru with her parents. She'd been ten and her father had been on a political goodwill tour of South America. The ambassador's wife had given her a small book of legends. The tale of a lost, highly developed civilization and their magic stones had captured her imagination, along with the notion that the stones had been handed down through a line of dark shamans who believed the stones held powers imbued by ancient interstellar visitors. The tale told that they had been hidden somewhere on an island by the last shaman of that ancient line, after a cataclysmic earthquake had wiped out the coastal tribes he had been bound to protect.

Whatever the truth of the stones' history, Nina had been fascinated. Trying to find them, discover if they truly existed, had become her life's work. She'd spent years studying the legends, the cultures, the evidence of primitive cataclysms and island superstitions. Finally she had narrowed her search to El Zarpa. A series of expeditions had led to hiring the guide who had taken her to the caves—and the find of a lifetime.

But now the stones were gone.

She felt as if she had a hangover, only there'd been no party. If it were actually possible, her head hurt more than it had the night before. The dull throb of pain stayed with her as she threw a thick robe over her pajamas and went downstairs. She needed coffee, and lots of it.

And she needed to get to work.

The thought of going back to the museum sent a trickling dread up her spine. She loved her work. She couldn't let anything stop her. Even her own fear.

In the meantime, she needed a locksmith. She couldn't stay on at her parents' house. They were expected back in a few days, and her relationship with them since the fraud allegations had come out had been uncomfortable, to say the least. The media's attention on the hoax theory had embarrassed them. She knew. They had told her frequently.

She went down the stairs, every step feeling as if she were taking it in a nightmare. The attack at the museum, the theft of the stones and her research, the ransacking of her apartment—

Riley.

He'd been *sweet* to her last night and that had been really hard to take. She wanted to hate him. The fact that she didn't wasn't the biggest problem in the surreal miasma of her life, but it wasn't her smallest, either, because his tenderness had lit a thousand nerve endings of hopeless need. Her feelings for him were much closer to the surface than she had fooled herself into believing.

She hadn't gotten over him. All these months later, and he was a raw, bleeding wound on her heart. It was pathetic, and it made her angry, at herself most of all.

She'd been so sure she could handle him, handle her emotions. She'd been a willing prisoner of their relationship, abandoning her pride for something she'd known deep down would go nowhere. He'd never mentioned love or family or marriage, or even a future.

She hadn't asked him for any of that, either. She'd had some idea that if she just held on long enough, she'd earn his love.

That hadn't happened. So why was he still inside her like a drug she couldn't get out of her system? It was high time to be done with Riley. Time for rehab—starting today.

Feeling better for having made that vow, she walked head high into her mother's kitchen. It looked like a display at a home decorating store—Tuscan tile, gleaming granite, polished stainless steel, all cleaned and shined to perfection. Not that her mother had anything to do with its pristine condition. She had a housekeeper, who was blessedly away while her parents were out of town.

Nina grabbed the citywide phonebook from the neat drawer by the fridge and thumbed through the pages for the locksmiths. If Riley'd been trying to make her paranoid, he'd done a good job. She called three before she found one who said he could be there around lunchtime.

Mozart played from the purse she'd left on the counter last night. She dashed and rummaged for the button.

"Nina! Are you okay? I've been so worried about you! I tried your apartment. Where are you?"

It was Juliet. Her assistant's usual bouncy energy came across in frantic worry this morning. "I'm at my parents' house. Did someone call you from the institute, or is this on the news already?"

"It's in the papers and on TV. Local and cable. Why are you at your parents' house?"

Nina's heart sank and the hard ball in her stomach ached. She grabbed the remote to the mini plasma TV her parents had hung on the wall over the kitchen table and punched it on, skipping through channels until she found one of the twenty-four-hour news networks. "My apartment was broken into last night before I got back home. My apartment keys were taken at the museum, so I couldn't spend the night there."

The screen showed a correspondent covering a train wreck in the Midwest. She flicked to the next cable news network, and her knees went weak. The clip was of her, from several weeks ago, when the news had broken about the fraud allegations. The coverage bounced to a talking head.

"—now infamous El Zarpa stones have gone missing from the institute and the truth about their origins may never be—"

"Nina? Nina?"

Juliet's voice dragged her back. "I'm here."

The screen switched to another talking head.

"Serious questions remain about the truth behind Dr. Phillips' research—"

"My God, are you all right?" Juliet demanded.

"—Dr. Phillips has been unavailable for comment since—"

When she didn't answer immediately, Juliet came at her again. "Do you want me to go with you back to the apartment?"

"No!" Nina hadn't meant that to come out so strongly, and she struggled to regroup. Juliet was all of twenty-two, glowing with excitement for her barely begun career and sexily hip with her swingy dark hair and high sun-kissed olive cheekbones. On a good day, she made Nina feel plain, and this was not a good day. "Thank you," Nina managed. "But I'm fine. I'm meeting a locksmith over there at noon."

"I'm so sorry about the stones," Juliet said. "I wish I wasn't going out of town. I'll cancel my plans if you want. I hate to leave with all this happening. You've worked so hard. I know how much they mean to you. I just can't believe they're gone."

Nina couldn't believe it, either, and maybe no one could relate as much as Juliet, who had worked with her so closely. She'd joined the institute staff shortly after the final expedition when Nina had brought the stones back to the States.

"Thank you," Nina said, choking up in spite of her desire to maintain her cool professional image. "But please don't change your vacation plans. There's nothing you can do here, and I'm fine. I have to go now," she lied.

The news channel switched to coverage of the train disaster. Nina sank onto one of the kitchen chairs.

The music started up again on her cell phone. The display showed the call was coming from the institute.

"Nina? Avano here."

She felt the dread rise in her throat.

"Has there been any word about the stones?" she asked quickly. Her heart pounded hard. She wanted news, good news. Desperately.

"We don't know anything further yet. I expect the police will be here shortly. Nina, I want you to stay home today." His voice was gentle but firm. He'd been something of a father figure to her in terms of her career, and ordinarily she was open to his advice.

Not today.

"No. I'll be in as soon as I can—"

"I'm afraid you don't understand, Dr. Phillips."

She swallowed over the sudden lump of fear in her throat. He never called her Dr. Phillips. She'd been nineteen when she'd first met Richard Avano. She'd started out as a docent at the museum, and her incessant questions and curiosity had led to an assistantship and eventually a research position at the institute. None of it would have happened if Dr. Avano hadn't taken an interest in her work and supported her one hundred percent.

"I'm fine, honestly," she rushed on.

"The media is all over us," Avano said over her protest. "We've got ten reporters here and a dozen more on the phone."

She had to fight back the urge to apologize for the ruckus. This wasn't her fault. "I'll be there as soon as I can. I'll—"

"I'm sorry to inform you that the board has requested that you be placed on administrative leave until the investigation has been concluded."

Shock rolled over in a cold wave.

"But—"

"We're a public institution, Dr. Phillips. We can't afford the merest whisper of misconduct and there are more than whispers. If I hadn't fought for you with the board, you would have been on suspension already. The hoax charges have severely tarnished the institute's reputation, and now with the stones gone..."

He didn't have to finish. She was a suspect. There were plenty of people who thought the stones were fakes, and now they thought she'd gotten rid of them to hide her fraud.

She'd thought the museum would back her. Dr. Avano had backed her. But the board hadn't.

"I didn't steal the stones. And they aren't fakes. When—" She nearly choked on that word. *When.* She couldn't bear to think in terms of *if* yet. "When we get the stones back, I'll prove it." She already had a geomorphologist set to authenticate them. All she needed were the stones, and time. More time. "I'd like the opportunity to speak to the board. I deserve to be heard."

This was her whole life. *Her career* was her whole life. She felt as if a Mack truck had just slammed into her. No, that had been last night when she'd realized the stones were gone. Today, the truck was backing up, driving over her again for good measure.

"I'm sorry, Dr. Phillips, but the board has no plans at this time to meet with you. Should that change, you'll be notified. Until further notice, you're not to set foot on institute property."

Museums, memorials and government headquarters slid by as Riley negotiated the heavily trafficked avenues of Washington, making his way toward PAX. He turned into the entrance and stopped at the security station. The guard at the gate waved him through to the underground parking garage.

The call had come in just after four. He'd had one hour to tie up the investigation and turn it over to another lead. He was off the case due to his ties with a "person of interest" in the case.

He left his car and strode quickly toward the parking garage elevator. The doors opened immediately, closing behind him as he stepped inside. Riley leaned into the seemingly innocuous, unmarked panel that held the bioread technology. Placing one eye level with the pinprick-sized camera installed in the panel, he gave it the second it took to digitally calculate the position, orientation and spatial frequency of his iris while the face scan matched his biometric characteristics against PAX's top secret database. He placed his palm against the fingerprint sensor.

Rather than heading up to the ten marked floors that made up the PAX League's offices that were open to the public, the elevator glided soundlessly, automatically, downward. Seconds later, the doors opened onto the main floor of the secret layer of the PAX League—the offices, laboratories, conference rooms and covert headquarters dedicated to leading the world into a new era of defense against global terror.

A security station lay central to the compact lobby, the bank of surveillance equipment lining the walls of the glassed-in office. Riley waited for the officer to visually ID him and then return to viewing the various monitors.

He headed straight for the office of Harrison Beck. He'd called ahead and the secretary told him the PAX chief was expecting him. Riley opened the door to find the chief sitting behind a massive desk in the dark, the flicker of a videotape illuminating his granite-profiled face.

Beck hit the Pause button as he looked up. "Sit down, Tremaine."

The tape restarted and Nina's face came onto the screen in footage Riley realized had to be from months ago, when the El Zarpa stones had first hit the news.

"Shamans were important in the South American social order because they had the power to access the spirit world." Nina's clear, authoritative voice filled the windowless PAX office. "The first shamans were believed to be gods and could control everything from the weather to the disposition of souls in the afterlife. There is a school of belief that the first shamans came from another planet. Such belief systems are fueled by the Nazca lines in Peru, which some believe to be prehistoric spaceports for aliens who once inhabited Earth. Of course, these theories are widely considered to be eccentric, but the mystery of the El Zarpa stones can only add to our understanding of ancient man's knowledge and where he may have come by it."

Nina went on to explain that anthropologists had

found evidence ancient man believed that upon the departure of these prehistoric aliens, they had left behind a library of their knowledge in the form of the El Zarpa stones. If ancient aliens weren't responsible for the stones, who was? This was the core of Nina's research. How could ancient man carve such technological wonders? And what did the shamans do with the stones and why were they hidden for centuries in caves on the remote island of El Zarpa? Who really carved the stones and when?

The excitement in Nina's face was palpable even through the video clips. She'd believed in her dream of finding the stones and, through her determination, had convinced the museum to underwrite her expeditions to the island nation of El Zarpa to allow her access to its most remote areas. El Zarpa was a poor and backward island, its topography unwelcoming.

The El Zarpan government had welcomed Nina, however. And then it had completely turned on her a few months later, denouncing the stones as fakes, foisting her guide, an illiterate, bedraggled native named Octavio Montoya, on the media to tell his story. Montoya claimed he'd carved the stones himself and Dr. Phillips had been in collusion with him on the hoax.

Guilty or innocent, Nina was in serious trouble. The investigation thus far revealed a likely inside job and she had the motive. Clearly, support for Nina at the institute had waned, based on the fact that she'd been put on leave from the museum. The question in most minds now wasn't whether she'd done it, but if she'd done it alone.

Top museum security officer Danny Emery had been found with a bullet in his head in Rock Creek Park an hour earlier, a suicide note at his side. The note claimed he'd done everything for Nina, a cryptic goodbye leaving investigators wondering just what he'd done for the institute anthropologist—if it had been the suicide, or some kind of participation in the robbery.

Beck moved on to another clip, this one of Nina, head bowed, running from the museum to her car, chased by reporters demanding answers. Riley could see her strong will in the haunted eyes she finally lifted her face to the cameras for one awful beat.

He felt himself sucked into her eyes, even through the videotape. She elicited pure emotion inside him, always had. She'd broken the fabric of his tidy life the day he'd met her, and it had never mended. All his adult life, he'd sought the companionship of women who didn't require emotional commitments. He'd allowed himself to slide into Nina's life on the belief that she, too, was one of those women simply because she made no overt demands. But he'd known that beneath that exterior independence, she was different.

She'd needed him, but she'd refused to admit it. And he'd almost let himself need her, too. Now he needed to protect her, and he needed emotional distance in order to do it.

The chief hit the remote's Pause button as Nina glanced back. The camera caught the proud and beautiful pain of her expression. Beck rose and moved around the desk to flick on the overhead light.

"We know there is a small, radical group with South American ties now operating under the direction of Eduardo Cristobal," he said, naming a man Riley knew had once been considered a brilliant Peruvian philosopher. His political beliefs had crossed the line to extremism and had put him on an international watch list. In a series of threatening speeches, he'd denounced what he called the U.S. cultural invasion of traditional South American society. Beck sat down behind his desk again. "We believe he was responsible for the deaths of two aid workers near Lima last year, not long after he went underground, as well as other terror incidents."

Cristobal had come to PAX's attention in the darkest hour of the League's history. They suspected it was operatives from one of Cristobal's cells who had infiltrated the organization via its highest officer. Serums created by PAX to empower a PAX agent with the strength, eyesight and speed of a wolf had nearly landed in the wrong hands. Cristobal's drive to revive ancient Andean culture had twisted into a desire to position himself as a shaman on the level of the lost gods.

While PAX had vetted a new chief and undertaken increased organization and greater levels of security and safeguards, Cristobal had become its most wanted terror mastermind.

Beck looked at Riley with his sharp amber-flecked brown eyes. His cropped gray hair reminded Riley of his military roots. Beck had been a decorated five-star general before taking on the leadership of PAX. "It's possible Cristobal is now engaged in some effort to gain control of antiquities with potential spiritual powers."

Riley had already communicated the visions he'd been experiencing—volcanoes, earthquakes and the sensation of evil centering around the institute and Nina.

"It's also possible," Beck continued, "that Cristobal had nothing to do with this theft whatsoever and that Dr. Phillips got rid of the stones to cover up her fraud. Or if Cristobal is involved, Dr. Phillips could be his link."

Riley gut tightened. "I don't believe that's the case, sir."

Beck waved a quick hand. "It's also possible," he went on, "that your visions are skewed by your personal history with this woman."

"I was taken off the case by the department an hour ago." Frustration burned hot in Riley's gut. "Dr. Phillips is innocent. And if what I'm seeing is real—"

Beck held up his hand. "I agree the threat is credible, given our knowledge of Cristobal's aims, and your personal history with Dr. Phillips could be of value. Intelligence is working to analyze the latest chatter for anything that could relate to this case. We have a team inside Peru working to pinpoint Cristobal's base, and they have a lead. We know he's changed his base more than once and tracking him has been difficult, but we believe we're closing in."

"I need some background checks," Riley said. The police department was conducting criminal checks on everyone employed at the institute, but he wanted more. "Someone at the museum has a link to Cristobal." He turned over copies of employee records he'd filed at the department.

Beck's hand closed over the documents and he slid them across the desk. "If Dr. Phillips is innocent, we need to know everything she knows about these stones, what her expert understanding of pre-Columbian anthropology would suggest about their use and possible alignment. And if she's guilty or in any way connected to Cristobal, we need to know that, too. She trusts you. Stay on her."

For a moment, Riley was relieved that he wasn't

being taken off the case by PAX, too. But it was clear Beck wasn't sure about Riley's visions. Or Nina.

"We believe," Beck continued, "that there's a possibility Dr. Phillips is in danger even if she's innocent. If Cristobal is behind the theft, he may need more than the stones. He may need Dr. Phillips. If there's an alignment, he'll be working as quickly as possible to figure it out and he may think Dr. Phillips can help. If your visions are wrong, this might be nothing. But if they're right, we can't risk losing her."

Riley hadn't seen Nina all day. He'd checked in with her at her apartment earlier, after learning she'd been put on administrative leave. He'd reassured himself that she had indeed had her locks changed. And maybe he'd wanted to hear her voice, too.

Dread twisted his stomach.

Riley shoved his chair back, urgency and adrenaline burning through his veins. He tasted danger. Not for himself, but for Nina.

"Stay in contact," Beck reminded him. "And don't let Dr. Phillips out of your sight."

Chapter 7

Nina took a cab back to the apartment to meet the locksmith and then spent a few hours trying to straighten up her ransacked apartment. Even with the locks changed, the apartment closed in on her, and she found herself jumping at every shadow. The sick sense of violation hung heavy in her stomach. The phone rang nonstop and she hadn't picked it up except for Riley's call. She'd assured him she'd had her locks changed and had asked him if she was going to need an attorney.

There had been a long pause, and he'd said, *It's possible.* After she'd hung up, she'd listened to five more reporters leave messages. When she couldn't take it anymore, she grabbed her spare car keys and headed for the museum. They might not want her to set foot on institute property but she'd be damned if she was going to go without her car. The cab let her out by the guard post. Apparently the guard didn't know about the board's decision since he waved her by with a somewhat quizzical look at the way she'd arrived.

There was a TV station van parked at the side of the museum and all she could think about was getting in, getting her car and getting the hell out of there before anyone asked her any questions. The parking lot was blessedly quiet.

The day was darkening rapidly with the threat of another storm. The stress and having had too little sleep were catching up with her and she had to force herself to focus on the road. A car beeped its horn behind her and she realized she'd completely lost track of time at a stoplight. All she needed now on top of everything else was to get into an accident. She left the heavily congested avenues for a patchwork route of side streets. The first splotches of rain hit her windshield.

She was halfway home, the sky opening up in earnest now, when she realized a black Yukon had been behind her the whole way. Adrenaline flooded her limbs. Who would follow her?

Turning down another side street, she watched in

the rearview mirror as the Yukon followed suit. Then she realized she'd turned down a one-way street—the wrong way. Parked cars lined the narrow street and a furniture delivery truck blocked the road, the driver laying on the horn to express his displeasure.

Behind her, she saw the Yukon's driver leap out of the vehicle and run toward her car through the hurling rain.

Her pulse pounded in her ears. She slammed the locks. There was something in his hand. Oh God, he had a gun. He was going to kill her. Another man burst from the other side of the Yukon.

A scream choked in her throat and she threw a panicked look at the truck driver. Then she swerved back to find the driver of the Yukon outside her car window.

Her heart just about leaped out of her chest when she realized he was holding a microphone. Not a gun. A microphone.

The man pounded on the window. Rain sluiced down his chiseled TV news-handsome face. "Channel 2 Flash News!" he shouted. "What can you tell us about the missing stones, Dr. Phillips? Did you steal them from the institute as a result of the fraud charges? Is this a cover-up? Is it true that an arrest warrant has been prepared in your name?" The man peppered her with questions through the glass. The other man propped a camera on his shoulder, zeroing in on her.

An arrest warrant? Horror rose in her throat.

"Do you have a comment on the suicide of the museum security chief, Danny Emery?" the reporter went on.

It took a full fifteen seconds for the man's words to sink in. *Danny was dead?*

Her mind reeling, Nina slammed the car into gear, making a tight three-point turn and nearly sideswiping three parked cars. Traffic continued to back up and when she scraped past the Yukon's fender, damaging its paint job as well as her own, she didn't care. She had insurance for a reason. So much for her perfect citizenship. She had to be losing her mind. She'd actually thought someone was coming after her on the street with a gun!

Her hands shook on the wheel and her heart raced. She zoomed down the street to her building, swept into the underground garage, leaving the pounding rain and reporters behind. She didn't look back. There was a security code at the entrance to the garage—they couldn't follow her here. Of course, they could get out and come inside the building, but she could refuse to open her apartment door.

She punched the elevator button and stepped inside. The elevator car whisked her upward and for the first time all day, she didn't care that her apartment could still qualify for federal disaster aid. She wanted to hide.

The locks were changed. Violated or not, she was safe here. *Until the police arrived with an arrest warrant.* Surely the reporter had made that up. He had to have been looking to get a sensational sound bite out of her. He couldn't have known that, could he?

And it couldn't be true, could it? What about what he'd said about Danny?

She pushed the door open, tucking it shut with her foot. The keys slid across the hall table as she tossed them. She left her raincoat on the hook by the door with her purse.

It was still early, despite the looming darkness outside. Most of the residents in her building worked, many of them in various government offices. The building was quiet. She flipped on the kitchen light and assessed the situation. She'd gotten her bedroom cleaned up and most of her office, but the living room and kitchen were still wrecked. She couldn't dredge up one shred of emotion for the shattered sea glass collection, or the energy it would take to clean it up.

The phone rang and she nearly jumped out of her skin. The machine picked up.

"Nina, it's Riley."

Her heart jumped into her throat. Her hand was cold as she grabbed the phone.

"Is Danny really dead?"

A taut beat. "Yes."

Oh God. This was a nightmare, and she was trapped in the center of it.

"I'm on my way," he went on. "We need to talk."

She shouldn't have picked up. She didn't want to talk. Maybe she never wanted to talk again. Every time she talked to someone, they told her something else she didn't want to know. And Riley— She'd promised herself just that morning to forget about him, yet even now, she couldn't bury her need for him. He made her feel safe, and she wanted desperately to feel safe right now.

But he made her feel other things, too, and she couldn't bear those other things. He'd torn a hole in her heart once, and if she let him back in now, he'd only tear a new one. Because he would leave her again. She was sure of that.

"Do you have an arrest warrant for me?"

"What? No."

She squeezed her eyes shut for a relieved beat. "Can you wait till later, then?" she asked finally. God, her legs were shaking. "I have every intention of cooperating with the investigation. I want the stones back more than anyone. But if you don't mind, I haven't had much sleep and I'm contemplating a coma at the moment. I'm sorry." She hung up without waiting for his answer and congratulated herself for not begging him to come right over this very second and never go away.

She remembered that she hadn't eaten since... She couldn't remember.

The thought of food turned her stomach, but she decided to try to force something down. Soup, maybe.

She threw open the pantry and took out a can of beef stew. Heating it seemed to take more effort than it was worth. She pulled off the lid and sat down with a spoon at the small table. She managed three bites of thick, cold stew straight from the can before she decided there was a reason people heated it up.

The phone rang again and she let the machine take it.

"Nina, I tried your office. Pick up this phone right now."

A ball of ice built in her chest. She reached for the phone. "Hi, Dad."

There was a long sigh—of relief of frustration, she couldn't tell—on the other end of the phone. Her temples throbbed.

"I'm halfway across the world and I've had six phone calls today about my daughter," Jackson Phillips complained. "Six, Nina. And a reporter caught me in front of the hotel this morning. What do you think he wanted to talk about? I'm here on trade issues and I'm fielding questions about whether or not my daughter is going to be arrested."

How are you, Nina? Were you injured? Are you scared?

"I'm not going to be arrested," she said tightly, knowing her father was never going to ask the questions she needed him to ask. God, her life was turning into a tabloid. Soon people would be claiming she'd had an affair with Danny Emery. And the senator would be the first to believe the story.

"What happened at the institute last night? How could you let those stones be stolen right out from under your nose? How are you going to prove they're not a hoax now?"

"Do you actually expect me to have answers to those questions, Dad?" Hot emotion stung her eyes. Why did she always feel as if she were eight years old and spilling milk at a dinner party when she talked to her father? "I'm doing the best I can. The police are doing the best they can."

"That's not good enough. I expect more from you. I expect—"

She wasn't good enough. This information wasn't new, but it stung just the same. She held the phone away from her ear until the cold diatribe coming out of it stopped.

Putting the phone back to her ear, she found the line silent. "Dad?"

"It's me, dear," her mother's voice responded. "Listen, we've got to run, but I wanted to ask you something while I've got you on the phone. I found this adorable shop with cherry jewelry boxes.

They're hand-engraved with embossed brass handles. I've never seen anything like them. I bought one for myself yesterday and I could go back and get one for you, if you'd like. It could be for your birthday."

Nina swallowed the lump in her throat. "That's okay, Mom. I already have a jewelry box."

Her mother hesitated. "You're all right, aren't you, dear?"

Tears pricked her eyes. "I'm fine."

It was the answer her mother wanted to hear. It was her way, and she'd accepted a long time ago that her parents would never change. Her father ordered problems fixed and expected his will to be done. Her mother pretended there were no problems to begin with. Then everyone could pose for a lovely campaign photograph.

Nina hung up the phone. When her parents returned to D.C. in two days, she would be no closer to them than she was now when they were in Europe.

It was no surprise that she had no idea how to be close to another human being. And yet, she knew that was no excuse. She was an adult. She was in control of her own actions. Still, she'd never felt more out of control in her life.

The phone rang again. The machine beeped on.

"Dr. Phillips, this is Brent Damien from Sky Cable News. We need your comment on the missing El Zarpa stones." He left a number for her to call him back.

That was not going to happen. She disconnected the phone cord and headed down the hall. She stopped in her office and pulled that phone cord, too. Her bedroom door was open and she stood in the opening, staring in at the room. She'd cleaned it up, but it still creeped her out. Someone had been in her room, touched her things. She wanted to be tired enough not to care, but she wasn't.

The phone rang again.

Before she could take a step, ready to disconnect that cord, too, something in the shadows of her darkened bedroom moved. Adrenaline bolted through her and she tore back down the hall.

But not fast enough.

The scream that came from Nina's apartment was one of pure terror. Riley's blood froze in his veins.

He used one powerful kick to blow the door down, his searching gaze zeroing on two shadows in the living room.

Nina wasn't screaming anymore. The attacker had one hand over her mouth; his other arm was brutally shoving her in the back as Riley burst in. Nina's wild eyes connected with Riley's, as did the attacker's. The man shoved Nina, pushing her to her knees, as Riley raced toward him. He grabbed the attacker, slammed a fist into his face. The man flew backward, hitting the mantel so hard he jarred loose a small vase. It shattered as it hit the floor, and the man reached for a lamp from a nearby table and threw it at Riley. Nina scrambled out of the way, screaming his name. Riley swerved out of the lamp's path. The attacker bolted for the balcony door, shoved it open and threw himself over the rail.

"Call 911," Riley shouted, racing after the man, who was already dropping past the next floor. He grappled for the second-floor railing, missed and fell.

His body hit the wet pavement and didn't move.

Nina ran out onto the balcony. "I called the police. What happ—" She stopped, face pale, staring down at the still man for a second before she backed into the balcony door. The phone in her hand hit the floor. Lost eyes stabbed him. He should be out of here, this second, securing the scene around the body.

No way was he leaving Nina. He wanted to hold her, keep her safe, and his fist curled into a ball at his side. There was danger tripping through his blood, more than physical danger.

"Did he hurt you, Nina?"

She stared at him for a long beat, as if she could barely understand what he was saying. She was in shock, he knew, and all he could think was that it was a good thing that guy was already dead because if he'd hurt Nina, Riley would have killed him with his bare hands.

"I'm okay. I had the locks changed," she added, confusion spiking her voice. Wind whipped in on the balcony, sweeping her hair off her pale cheeks. "I don't know how he got in. He was waiting for me in the bedroom."

But she wasn't okay, far from it. Her quiet devastation broke the remnants of his restraint. He didn't hesitate, just pulled her into his arms, felt the solid reality of her, breathed with relief that she was still alive.

Sobs shook her body, and he held her tightly, realizing he was shaking almost as badly as her. He didn't want to ever let go. He could feel her heart pounding, same as his, and he held her, caressed her hair, her back.

"Thank you," she whispered against his chest. "If you hadn't been here— If you hadn't—"

"I'm here." He held her tighter. She could have died, or been kidnapped. He had to close his eyes for a moment, overwhelmed by the keening sense of grief and fear that swamped his emotions.

He was still rubbing her shoulders, and the scent of her hair came to him as he trailed his fingers through its tangled silk. The urge to pull her even closer blindsided him. He'd forgotten how it felt to need someone else this way. Forgotten how it felt to need anything outside of his mission.

"I'm not going to let anything happen to you," he

declared huskily. He opened his eyes, gazed down at her bowed head against his chest. "Nobody's going to hurt you. Nobody." The ferocity of his own vow shook his world. He wanted to take away her fear, her pain.

She moved against him, and he tried desperately to deny the coiling desire shocking his senses. She was scared. He was there to protect her. She was his assignment.

But none of that had anything to do with what he was feeling now. And the dangerous truth of the moment overpowered all logic.

She lifted her face toward him, her eyes wide and dark and aching with a want as fierce as his. She needed his touch as much as he needed hers. Her mouth was a whisper away and before he could think, he crushed his lips to hers. Her response was soft and sweet and hot. The low, soul-shattering sound she made in her throat shot the crumbling remainders of his discipline to hell. She opened her mouth to him, and he instantly deepened the kiss, sweeping his tongue into her mouth as she looped her arms around his neck.

Heart thundering, he kissed her, touching her neck, her shoulders, her back, his fingers sliding beneath her shirt and skimming the bare curve of her waist. She felt breathtakingly alive, and he poured thirteen months of loss into their kiss, letting himself feel things he'd refused to acknowledge until tonight. His mind and his body melded into one hot sensation as he drank from her as if he were dying of thirst.

He didn't want this precious moment to stop but he heard a sound like a choked sob catch in her throat. Dizzy with the desire exploding inside him, he tore his mouth from hers, afraid he'd gone too far, taken too much.

She gazed up at him in the shadowed room, her eyes huge, her lips swollen and wet.

There was a new shock in her eyes, and maybe a flicker of panic, but she wasn't pulling away, wasn't running. Their gazes held.

Nina stared into Riley's eyes, wondering wildly what there was about this one man that made her drop all her defenses so easily. Dear God, she'd kissed him. He'd kissed her with just as much abandon and need, and that fact only served to confuse her more. And now—

Now there was an odd mix of regret and passion in his eyes that broke her heart.

"Nina—" he started.

"Don't be sorry," she broke in shakily. She took a deep breath. "I was scared and—" She had a right to be scared. Terrified. It wasn't a real excuse for what they'd just done, but she'd take what she could get.

A tremor shook her as she looked around, through the balcony door to the ransacked state of her living room. "Just don't go anywhere," she added softly.

"I'm not leaving you alone." His dark eyes burned with a worry—for her—that clutched at her heart. She could see him struggling as desperately as she was to regain control. "You can't stay here anymore. We think—" He shifted his hold, put some distance between them. "There's a good chance the people behind the theft of the stones need more than the stones. They may think they need you."

"Why?" Fear rippled through her again and she didn't want any distance. She wanted him to hold her tightly again, but she was scared of that, too.

"The theft was an inside job," he said, not answering her question yet. "There's no evidence anyone outside the secure areas broke into the museum."

"Danny? Why would Danny do that?"

"He left a note that seems to take the blame for the theft of the stones, said he did everything for you."

Shock spun through her. "For me? He was sorry for me when the fraud charges came out, I know that. He was kind to me, kinder than most people. But— I didn't really know him very well. I mean, we'd say hello and he'd always tell me to be careful, in a fatherly sort of way. He was always giving safety tips to the women at the institute, especially the ones he knew were single, like me. And Juliet. He always walked Juliet out, too—she'd had a horrible experience with a boyfriend who stalked her several years ago. But—" A thought suddenly hit her. "Why would he knock me out if he was doing it *for* me?"

"To protect you?" Riley suggested. "The fact is, we don't think we have the full story. And we're not sure it's really a suicide. The note hasn't been authenticated yet."

Nina pressed shaking fingers to her mouth.

"Even though the theft itself was an inside job, we believe there is someone else behind the crime. Where are the stones if that's all there is to it? There's a group of fanatical extremists in South America who believe in the magic of the lost shamans. They're terrorists, Nina. It's possible they're after the power of the El Zarpa stones. And that's why they want you."

She felt the hairs rise on the back of her neck.

"That's just a legend," she breathed harshly. "That's crazy."

"I didn't say these people were sane."

The hard depth of his stare shook her to her core. The stark realization of the danger she could be in, simply for having discovered the stones and studied them, hit her at the same time that she was struck by a keen sense of relief. The police believed her, then. They knew she wasn't behind the theft.

"That's why you can't stay here anymore," he said grimly. "It's not safe." His gaze swept the building, then pierced the rainy gloom of the alley below.

He swore hotly under his breath even as an officer called from the doorway of her apartment. "He's not dead!" Riley exclaimed. "Tell them he's not dead!" Before she could speak, he dived over the railing.

Chapter 8

"Do something!" Nina demanded, frustration spiking her blood. The officer had been in her apartment for five full minutes—five minutes that felt like five hours—and he hadn't done a damn thing but speak into his phone and walk out to the balcony. He'd sent his partner down to look for Riley and her attacker, but she wanted more.

"We sent a unit around to the side of the building for backup, ma'am. If there was an intruder here in your apartment, it's my job to stay here for your protection until we've got the situation under control."

"If?"

"Your door's busted down, but you're saying Detective Tremaine did that. I don't see any other sign of forced entry, ma'am. You had an incident here last night. There was no sign of forced entry then, either."

"No, but—"

The officer's radio beeped. Nina rose, restless, to pace to the balcony again. The alley was completely dark, the wind cold. Where was Riley? And why was this police officer treating her as if she were the criminal?

"Ma'am."

She turned back.

"My partner caught up with Tremaine. There's no sign of the intruder."

"Is Riley okay?" she asked quickly.

The officer watched her for a beat. "Detective Tremaine's fine, ma'am. He'll be up in a minute with my partner. Now, you want to tell me again what happened?"

He had a small pad and wrote down the bare details as she repeated her story. She broke off as Riley and the other officer appeared at the door.

"I lost him," Riley said when she made a beeline for him. He was soaked, hair matted to his head, rain dripping off his jacket. His eyes looked nearly black.

The other officer, wet as well, stared past them toward his partner. "Didn't see a sign of anyone," he said.

"No sign of forced entry here," the first officer repeated. "That's two incidents, well, three if you count the museum, with no evidence of intrusion, ma'am."

He flipped the notebook shut.

They thought she'd made it up. They thought this was a hoax. *Another* hoax.

Nina opened her mouth to speak, anger welling, but Riley beat her to it, his face darkening dangerously as he stalked past her toward the officer.

"There *was* an intruder." Riley's voice came out like cut glass. "I saw him. I fought with him. He got away, went over the railing. That's when we put the call in to the police. I thought he was dead, or out cold. I was worried about Dr. Phillips' safety and I didn't want to leave her alone in her apartment, but when I saw him get up, I took off after him."

"What were you doing here anyway?" the officer asked Riley. "You're off the case, Tremaine. Did you forget that?"

The breath jammed in Nina's throat. Her head reeled again.

"Off the case?" she repeated, her gaze slamming into Riley's. Why hadn't he told her that? He'd spoken about the case as if he were still on it.

"We'll take another look around," the other officer said. "And we've notified the unit doing patrols in this area. In the meantime, you want to be sure you have this door fixed, ma'am. It's not safe."

"What are they talking about, off the case?" she said again. She forgot about the other officers. She didn't care that they were leaving. They weren't going to do a damn thing to help her, anyway. She needed Riley on so many levels, and the strain of fighting that need had her snapping.

"You told me the police believed in me," she spat at him. They were alone now, the door propped in place by the officers as they'd left. "You told me— What is this story about *we* think this and *we* think that? Terrorists are after the El Zarpa stones. Terrorists are after me. Those police officers didn't say anything about that. It doesn't even sound like—"

Riley's hollow eyes shot a twist of fear down her spine. He strode toward her, impatience in the air around him. "You're pale. You need to get out of here, and you need to rest."

"It doesn't sound like a job for the police," she whispered starkly. "Oh my God." The cool air wafting in from the still-open balcony door sent down her spine. "Who else are you working for?"

"There are some things you don't need to know, Nina."

She felt the ache of a chasm between them in the harsh mystery of his words, and she fought her way out of the morass of emotion that thought inspired. Her head throbbed wickedly, but she wasn't letting this go.

"How long has this been going on? How long have you been working for someone other than the police? When we...when we knew each other?"

Had she ever really known him? What did she know of him *now?* He was a mass of contradictions—gentle but enigmatic, safe but dangerous, honest but mysterious.

"No."

"Then when?"

"It doesn't matter."

"I think it does matter, or you wouldn't be avoiding the answer." She didn't know why it mattered to her. She didn't know why she was pushing. Something had gone terribly wrong between them, and her shattered heart still wanted to know what had happened.

And damn her heart for grasping at straws. But he'd kissed her. He'd been as hungry for her as she'd been for him. Yet he was clearly prepared to fight what felt so right and so real, and that hurt more than anything.

She'd been waiting her whole life to find something as real as what she'd found with Riley. It'd been real for him, too, she'd been sure of it. And the doubts of all these long months had just exploded in that kiss. But he'd fought it, and he was prepared to keep right on fighting it.

Or was she kidding herself again?

"Why are you off the case with the police?"

He closed the space between them, grasped her shoulders again and caught her gaze with fierce resolve. The carved lines of his face seemed deeper suddenly, his voice weary.

"You're a person of interest in the case. They know about our prior relationship. They think I can't be objective."

She didn't know whether to laugh or cry that the police thought he couldn't be objective about her. She didn't know what that meant. She didn't know what that kiss meant, but it couldn't mean—

"Who are you working for?" she repeated. She couldn't handle any of her other questions right now. "Do *they* believe me?"

His blue-black eyes burned into her. "I believe in you, Nina."

It wasn't an answer. Not a real one.

Oh God, these people he worked for, maybe they didn't believe her, either.

But the insane terrorists—they believed in her. They'd come here to get her. They'd taken her research, the stones, and now they wanted her.

Fear thumped in her chest. "They're going to come after me again," she whispered. The only man she had to turn to was full of secrets, and yet she still trusted him. But was that wise? Her heart warred with her mind, and she felt sick. Her life was at stake here. She had to focus on that one fact.

"I'm going to protect you." His hands still gripping her arms, he pulled her closer. "And in return, I need you to tell me everything you've discovered about the stones. There could be some kind of alignment to the stones that is the key to their power. I need to know how they could be used, anything that might give me a clue as to finding the people behind the theft."

She stared at him, dumbfounded. "I don't know anything about an alignment." Her life had gone insane, and she had no idea what he was talking about. And if she couldn't figure it out, maybe she wouldn't have a life left to worry about. *I'm going to protect you.*

His vow made her want to cry.

"There has to be a way," he insisted. "If you can recreate the images on the stones from memory—"

He stopped short at her sharp gasp.

She tore from his hold to her purse that was still, thank God, in the hall by her coat. She grabbed it and rummaged through, turned back to Riley. Keeping the disk a secret until she made a copy didn't seem to matter anymore, not when her life was at stake. Everything she had, everything she was, depended on Riley now, whether it was safe or wise or even right.

In the end, it didn't matter why he was helping her, that her heart shattered every time she looked at him, or that she wanted so much more from him than his protection. This was a matter of survival.

She held out the disk.

He tucked her into the passenger side of his car where he'd parked it in front of the building. Rain beat down on the roof, shrouding the vehicle in a stormy cocoon. While she'd gathered some things, he'd pulled out his phone and placed a call to Beck. The break-in would be investigated, her apartment secured. He'd gotten the name of the locksmith she'd used and transmitted that information.

"Where are we going?" Nina asked, turning her uncertain, wide eyes to him in the dark car. She wore a plain olive-green shirt with cargo pants. Her rain jacket was unzipped, revealing a line of pale throat. Her copper hair was tucked behind her ears. "I still have my parents' keys—"

"Everyone knows you're the senator's daughter," he said quietly. He hated to scare her, but she had to face the reality of her situation. "Last night, we didn't understand they wanted you, too. Now we do. We'd be putting your family and their home at risk to take you back there."

She chewed her lip, looking away, but not before he saw the flare of fear in her eyes. He would do anything to take that fear from her. His original plan had been to watch over her at her apartment, but that wasn't possible now. "For tonight, I'm taking you to a hotel."

"No." Her response was swift, her eyes flashing panic.

"I'll make sure you're safe." He'd plant himself outside her door.

"I don't want to go to a hotel." She shivered and wrapped her arms around her body. "There are too many people there, people with keys to the room. And there's the media. Someone will see me and call a reporter. They've been hounding me all day." The struggle to keep her voice from breaking was lost.

His heart was torn. She'd been through too much. "The only other place I can take you tonight is my apartment." His chest tightened and he felt the hellish need that was so wrong. Nina needed to feel safe, and she was wrong if she thought his apartment was anything near safe.

She was a danger to him, and that made him a danger to her. He couldn't shove his need for her into that black hole where he'd kept it for the past thirteen months, no matter how he tried. He'd lost control in her apartment, kissed her. And the ache inside him to kiss her again was so huge, it threatened all reason.

"Then let's go to your apartment," she said simply, looking at him with so much agonized trust that he was overwhelmed. She was putting her life in his hands the same way she'd turned over that disk she'd kept secret. She'd been scared, and he'd understood that, but now, when she was even more frightened, she'd given it to him.

He could only pray that it would quicken their understanding of what Cristobal wanted with the stones. His reaction to Nina, this bond that snapped between them still—it was all far too risky.

Rain slid down the dark car windows. Riley squeezed his eyes shut for a long beat. He would die for her, he knew. The emotion behind that knowledge was something he wasn't ready to face, but he had to face the truth of his need. He had to fight it.

He felt the pull of her sucking him under, and he could only pray he'd get through tonight without doing something she'd regret.

Keying the ignition, he pulled away from her building. He drove around, taking a circuitous route to his apartment, ensuring they weren't being followed. He couldn't guarantee no one would look for Nina at his place if they'd seen her leave with him, but as long as he was there with her, he wouldn't let anything happen to her.

His building was nothing like Nina's. In the less expensive city outskirts, he lived in a quiet, sprawling two-story complex with widely diverse tenants, from seniors to young families with children. His was a second-story, one-bedroom unit at the back.

He followed Nina up the outside stairs to his door. She remembered the way, and he remembered too keenly the last time he'd taken her there. It had been a week before the accident. It had been her birthday. He'd taken her out to dinner, given her a pair of earrings, brought her back to his apartment where they'd—

Shoving the key in the lock, he flipped the wall switch just inside the door and jammed the traitorous thoughts deep into the recesses of his tortured memory.

They were both soaked. Even though they'd worn jackets, their dash from the car had left their clothes wet. The door of his apartment opened immediately to the small living room. The apartment was decorated in what Nina had jokingly called "bachelor functional." There was a black futon in the living room and a TV big enough to watch football. The dining area held a small table he used for a desk and two folding chairs. There was a bar and a couple of stools in the tiny kitchen. One bedroom and a small bathroom connected through the far door.

"You're shivering," he said as she stood there, hesitating. "Why don't you get changed, and I'll fix you something to eat."

She nodded, gripping the small bag of overnight gear she'd gathered at her apartment. He set his keys down on the bar counter and closed the space between them. He reached for the collar of her jacket and pulled off her coat. She moved the overnight bag from one hand to the other as she slid her arms out of the sleeves, then turned and caught his gaze.

"Thanks."

He nodded, his entire body sensitized from the brush of her hair against his hands as he'd tugged off her jacket. The shirt she wore defined every curve of her breasts and waist, and the cargo pants clung damply to her legs. She reached up to rub her temples and he saw the bruise on the tender flesh of her inner arm he hadn't noticed before. Fingerprints of the man who had attacked her. Now, in the bright light of his apartment, he saw the faint marks on her cheeks where a hand had been clamped over her mouth.

She disappeared into the back while he searched for something quick to fix. He settled for canned chili and started heating it in a pan on the stove.

"Can I help?"

He turned to find Nina standing behind him, in a huge T-shirt and baggy sweatpants that did nothing to make her look any less sexy. She'd tied her hair back in a loose ponytail that left red-brown tendrils sweeping across her cheeks.

"You can eat," he said, dumping spoonfuls of chili into a serviceable bowl and pushing it across the bar counter toward her.

She'd brought the disk and had set it on the counter. He picked it up, intent on speeding the conclusion of this mission. He sat down at the desk in his dining room office and shoved it in the laptop. The machine hummed and a list of files appeared in the box on the screen.

He heard Nina move. He turned and saw her pull up the other folding chair. She stuck the bowl of chili to the side and leaned forward, taking over the keyboard. He noticed the way she bit at her lower lip as she concentrated. Her life was hell, but she was still strong.

"Those are the digital images." She began moving the files to his hard drive. He could smell chili and Nina's hair. He could hear breathing, slow and steady, over the rain and the hum of the computer. He could feel the heat of her nearness slide through his veins.

She sat back and picked up her bowl, watching him as he slid over, took the keyboard, dumped all the files into an e-mail and hit Send.

"Who are you sending them to?" she asked.

He looked at her.

"Oh," she said quietly. "I guess if you tell me, you have to kill me, right?"

There was a guarded look to her deep green eyes, though she met his gaze head-on, unblinking. It was the kind of offhand comment the old Nina would have made, the unexpected teasing sarcasm that was part of her all-too-serious charm.

His covert work was a topic far too dangerous to the distance he needed to keep between them. She was curious, and he couldn't blame her. But he couldn't satisfy her curiosity, either. Not if he wanted to have a hope in hell of keeping that distance. He'd put an end to their relationship for her sake, and he couldn't forget that.

What he needed was control. He'd been a victim of circumstances in his childhood, and he'd fought for control all his adult life. It had never been difficult to keep to himself, to protect others and shield his heart.

Not until Nina had come along. But PAX had come along, too. He'd woken in the hospital, weak and starkly depressed. He'd endured months of grueling physical and brain therapy, pushing himself to recover his strength and to train his mind to use the power he'd been given. He'd found his purpose, and there was no going back.

No matter how he still yearned for Nina.

"The more eyes on the stones now, the better," was all he said in response to her question about the e-mail. He turned back to the screen, switched to a software program where he could bring up the files he'd transferred.

He could want Nina till kingdom come, but he

couldn't do anything about it. Neither could he satisfy her curiosity about his secret work. But if they were lucky, he could save her life.

"Tell me about the stones," he said.

Chapter 9

"Stone can't be radiocarbon-dated," Nina explained. "Radiocarbon dating depends on organic material—something that was once alive—to reveal age. But look at the varnish."

She leaned forward, brushing his arm slightly as she pointed to one of the rocks on the screen. Her enthusiasm for her work, her amazing talent and precise control, strengthened her voice. She'd been out of her element for the past twenty-four hours, and now she was back in it. "The varnish on the stones comes from bacteria and tiny organisms attaching to the surface. It takes thousands of years for that to occur, and that the varnish is even in the grooves where the etchings appear indicates they are very old."

She traced the carvings in the stone on the screen. "If the stones were a hoax, the etchings wouldn't contain this varnish. I had a geomorphologist lined up to study them, but now—"

"Would a geomorphologist have been able to authenticate them?"

Nina sighed and sat back. "I don't know. I'd specifically asked her to provide findings on the varnish. The fraud charges were based on the varnish having been faked. The native who led me to the stones is claiming now that he carved them himself, but that's impossible." Her eyes flashed now, and he could see her damaged pride. "The man was illiterate, impoverished. There's no way he could have had the skills or knowledge to have pulled off a hoax like this, and I certainly would never have participated in it. The rocks are a form of andesite, a very hard volcanic material. Carving into them would be extremely difficult."

Riley disconnected from the pull of Nina's fierce pride to study the eleven stones on the screen again. Humans flying on the backs of pterodactyls filled one. Advanced surgeries, including heart transplants, were depicted on another. Several held maps of the world and the heavens in unfamiliar configurations. Each included a background of a man wearing a robe and adorned with a crown, holding what appeared to be a stone. Every stone held a different depiction, all revealing sophisticated knowledge of science and technology, the Earth and the cosmos. The shapes of the stones were odd, uneven, the etchings so fine they could have been done with a modern-day laser.

"What do you know of the stories about the stones?" he asked. "What were the stones supposed to do?"

"Legend has it the stones originated from ancient astronauts who brought them here to Earth. They were used for thousands of years by dark shamans, then hidden away by the last of that line," she explained. "There's nothing in the historical record to back up the stories about these particular shamans. Juliet, my assistant, has done extensive research for me into—"

"What does that mean, ancient astronauts?" Riley cut in.

"That part of the world has always been a center of spiritual fascination with the idea of interstellar visitors in ancient times," Nina told him. "The Nazca lines in Peru, for example, are even now widely believed to be the remains of some ancient spaceport because when viewed from space, the lines look like runways. The pull of the sea represents the creative flow, and electromagnetic energies are very strong in that part of the world. If man could harness that electromagnetic energy, somehow focus cognitive energy into the cosmos, that power could be captured to create catastrophic disturbances here on Earth. Volcanic eruptions, cataclysmic floods, disruptions of continental plates…"

As Riley focused on the images on the screen, the buzz of energy swept over him. He felt his mind leave his body, sucked into that dark vortex over which he had no control.

Wind swept a misty rise as a robe-draped hand aligned the stones and held one up to the heavens. Then Riley was blinded. The earth shook and fire roared over his body, engulfing him. Nina screamed—

He jolted back in his seat, the power of the stones' energy tingling through his veins.

A hand touched his arm, and he jerked around. Nina stared at him, her face pale, frightened.

"What's wrong?" she breathed.

He swallowed thickly, unable to speak.

"Are you okay?" There was a fragile thread to her voice. She was depending on him, and even though he'd left his body and come back within a second, the crackling heat of the mental transfer hung in the air.

He couldn't explain it to her, nor could he explain that it frightened him, too. Especially the part where he heard Nina's scream.

With a will honed by months of work in controlling his physical and emotional responses to the horror of the evil in his visions, he asked with painful control, "What would the shamans have done with the stones? What good could they produce?"

"They would have been used to capture healing energies, as well," she said, a slight uncertain shake still in her voice. "But most likely they were used to control people through fear. A catastrophic natural event occurs, and a shaman claims he produced the event through the stones. Someone is healed, same thing. The stones don't really have any power. The real mystery is in the complex knowledge held by whoever created them. That's the fascinating anthropological question."

She'd shoved aside the bowl of chili now.

"What was it you said about an alignment?" she asked.

Her eyes showed fatigue, but she was ready to work. She was fragile beneath that tough facade she was trying to put on now, though.

"Would the shamans have laid out the stones in a certain pattern? Would they have to be in a specific location to use the stones? Maybe an order to the pictures, or a way the stones themselves might interlock?"

She leaned forward again, scrutinized the screen. He noticed again the shadows under her eyes and the bruising on her cheek, the sweet scent of her hair and the soft slide of her breath.

"The stones could be divided into categories," she mused. "Medical, astronomical, technological, even the fantastical." She lifted her gaze to him again. "But if there was to be some type of alignment, it would be based on some celestial or geographic order. For instance, the lines of magnetic flux are higher in Peru than anywhere else in the world, so as for location, my first thought would be wherever the lines of flux are most intense." She rubbed her temples, and she sounded dead tired.

"You've had a rough twenty-four hours," he said. "The best thing you can do now is get some sleep."

In his bed. While he stretched out on the uncomfortable futon and stayed as far away from her—and the sweet, clean, sexy pull of her as possible. The short distance between them was killing him. What kind of man was he that he wanted her this much when she was hurting and exhausted?

"I'd rather work." She brushed the falling tendrils from her ponytail back behind her ears and turned back to the screen.

He knew what she was doing. She was throwing herself into her work, avoiding thinking about the rest of her currently messed-up life. He worked with her for a while, manipulating the digital images so that they could play with the stones, shifting them into endless configurations, until, impatient, she took over the keypad and mouse again.

She got up once to brush her teeth and wash her bowl out in the sink, but came right back to work. He must have been as tired as her, or maybe he just didn't have as much discipline as he thought he had, because when she sat down again, shoulders hunched, expression tense, as she stared into the screen again, it was all he could not to slide his hand behind her neck, down her back and gently knead the bunched muscles there.

Only that would be wrong because he would want to do more than make a comforting gesture. The throb low in his belly was proof of that, along with the hollow hunger in his heart that, until last night, he'd thought had been put out of working order permanently.

He got up before he could do any of the wrong things in his mind. He took as much time as possible in the bathroom, hoping she'd go to bed while he was gone.

When he came back, Nina's head was on her arms over the desk, her eyes closed. She looked achingly vulnerable and breathtakingly beautiful all at once.

He touched the side of her face. Her skin felt so soft, so smooth. Her lashes fluttered and she looked at him. He couldn't stop himself. He slid his hand back over her hair, one sweet touch that would never be enough. Something flared in her eyes, a need he recognized. It would be too easy in this moment to pull her into his arms.

"Hey," he breathed, forcing himself to move his hand back to his side.

"I just laid my head down for a minute," she said, pushing herself back up.

"You're exhausted."

"I have to work." She turned back to the screen.

"You have to sleep, Nina. Come on." He wasn't giving her any choice now. "You're going to make yourself sick." He doubted she'd slept the night before, at least not much. "Go to bed on your own or I'll carry you there."

His gentle threat lay heavy in the suddenly dangerous air. The moment stretched, and then she conceded defeat. "All right. But I can't take your bed."

"Yes, you can." He blocked her path as she rose.

She hesitated for an interminable beat. Something taut hummed in the air.

"I really don't want you to be so nice to me," she said, her chin hardening. "You saved my life. You're the only one who believes in me. You're doing everything you can to help me. And yet when you needed help..."

The past entered the charged atmosphere in the confused pain of her shimmering green depths. He didn't know where to begin to explain. He'd lied to her in the hospital. He'd still been a mess then, physically and emotionally. She'd been collateral damage.

"I'm sorry, Nina," he said roughly, knowing it wasn't enough.

She looked away for a long beat. He could see a pulse jump in her throat.

"Maybe you can't tell me this," she went on then, her voice heartbreakingly low, "and maybe I'm just kidding myself to think it's connected, but I'm so tired of being scared." Her shining eyes stabbed him again. "If sending me away had anything to do with this…secret work of yours, you're kidding yourself if you think you're doing me a favor to lie. You kissed me tonight, and if I could understand how you can do that and still treat me like a stranger, maybe it wouldn't hurt so much."

Guilt twisted, sharp and deep.

"Nina—"

"Unless you're going to tell me the truth, don't tell me anything at all," she whispered harshly. "Because you can't have it both ways. You can't lie to me and still kiss me. Maybe you can handle that, but I can't. Are you going to tell me the truth, Riley?"

He heard a heartbeat—hers or his, he had no idea. It pounded in his ears. She'd given him all her trust, not just now, but thirteen months ago. And he'd given her nothing. At least, nothing that cost him anything.

"That's what I thought," she said and even as he reached for her, she tore away, leaving him alone and feeling guilty as hell.

Nina shut the door of Riley's bedroom behind her with a force that shook the walls. The anger felt good. It overrode the pain and the fear. She ripped off the sweatpants that were uncomfortably baggy, threw them down on the bag of overnight things she'd brought. Hitting the switch on the lamp, she doused the room in darkness and climbed into Riley's bed.

The sheets smelled like him.

Light suddenly rayed in from the door. Riley stood silhouetted in the opening.

"I knocked but—" He hesitated there in the doorway, then stepped inside. As he neared her, she saw a mirror reflection of her own pain and need.

Time stood still for an awful beat. She'd admitted too much, and yet she wasn't sorry. She'd been fighting this need for him that went beyond her physical safety, and she was tired of fighting in the dark. Maybe she could get over him if she could just understand.

Or maybe she didn't want to get over him at all.

"You're right—I did lie to you in the hospital," he said suddenly into the raw silence of the room. "I never thought I was doing you a favor, though. I was doing myself a favor. I didn't think I was strong enough to tell you even a fraction of the truth and still walk away."

Nina didn't know whether her heart was falling apart or was whole for the first time in thirteen months. She just knew she didn't want him to stop talking.

She rose. "What is the truth?"

The shadow of him didn't move. "I'm not the same man I was before the accident, in more ways than I'm at liberty to tell you. I can't even tell you how it happened, or why, but it doesn't matter. What matters is that what I do now is dangerous. And that's why—"

The breath jammed in her throat. All the questions, the doubts of thirteen months, answered so simply and so painfully.

"I didn't want to put you in danger." His words were low, hard, threaded with self-recrimination.

"I *am* in danger."

In the darkness, his eyes gleamed bitterly. "I don't want to put you in *more* danger, Nina. I don't want to hurt you. I never wanted that." The strain of his voice shook her. "And if I didn't tell you the truth thirteen months ago, it was because I didn't have an ounce of the courage you have. God, Nina, I can't take one step more into this room because I know I'll hurt you again if I do, don't you see that?"

She stepped toward him. "Do you think it hurts me less *not* to know that? To think that you *don't* want me?" She came to a stop in front of him and in that short distance, she could feel his heat, his need.

"You don't need me in your bed, Nina," he said. "You're vulnerable. You're in trouble. You need help, not—" She could see him fisting his hands at his sides as if to stop himself from touching her. "The truth doesn't change anything."

But he was wrong. The truth changed everything. He was telling her there was no chance of a future for them, but she didn't know if she had a future at all.

Touching his chest, she felt his heart pounding. "I don't care."

She closed her eyes, tipped her face up, blindly reaching for his mouth.

The contact stunned her, instantaneous and undeniable. His mouth crushed hers and the hunger in it made her want to cry. His hands tangled in her hair and she found herself arching into him. She was lost—to reason, to sanity, to any hope of stopping.

She could feel the hard ridge of him against her stomach, and she remembered every brush, every touch, every sweeping, searing jitter of passion he unleashed. How she stayed standing, she didn't know, because he melted her to the bone. His kiss was fierce and gentle all at once. Her hands skimmed over his shoulders, feeling the heavy, bunched power of him as he held her against him. Arousal flooded through her and she poured all the months of grief and loneliness into the sheer sweet possession of it.

He wanted her. It wasn't pity, or comfort. It was passion. Her breasts grew heavy with forgotten need. She wanted to feel him inside her.

She wanted to feel alive.

Then a hard sound broke from his mouth and he drew back slowly. She stood there, shaking, the air thick between them. He met her eyes, letting her see all the fierce longing in them, letting her see that he wanted so much more. It wasn't one-sided, this hunger that went beyond any desire she'd ever known before. He felt it, too.

He took a step back, putting more distance between them, and drew a ragged breath. His eyes were so dark, so hopeless, and something inside her bled.

"I care enough for both of us," he said roughly. He turned away and shut the door.

Chapter 10

Riley washed his face in the sink of his small bathroom, trying not to notice the invasion of Nina even here. Her toothbrush, her comb, the small bottle of facewash that wove through his senses. It smelled like Nina, fresh and clean and faintly of apple and dreams.

He tried to slow down his heart, tame the beast he'd stupidly let loose in that bedroom. He'd kissed her. Not once, but twice, and he'd wanted to do a hell of a lot more. All Nina had to do was look at him with those green eyes of hers and he was lost; his mind blanked out his duty, both to PAX and to her. He was a disciplined man. He prided himself on it. The strength of his will was all that had dragged him out of the homeless poverty of a childhood empty of expectation and love.

Nina had offered him both, and it was a cruel irony that he couldn't accept them. But it was his job to protect her, even from himself. He'd promised her, he'd promised himself, that he would take care of her, that everything would be all right.

Trying not to think too hard about the chances of that, he walked out to the living room and sat on the lumpy futon he'd bought used at a thrift store. He pulled out his cell, placed a call to Beck and briefed him on the situation.

"We have the files you sent," Beck said. "They're under analysis right now. Have you had a chance to question Dr. Phillips about any theories she might have in regard to the stones?"

"Not thoroughly. She's pretty exhausted and frightened right now." And his control was crumbling, but Beck didn't need to know that. He was already walking a fine line with PAX on this mission. They didn't entirely trust him, and they didn't entirely trust Nina. And the hell of it was, he didn't entirely trust himself. "Possible location could be the magnetic lines of flux along the Peruvian coastline, or some other geographic or astrological positioning. What do we know about Danny Emery's death?"

"Powder tracings show it wasn't a suicide."

Riley digested that information.

"What about the assistant, Juliet Manet?" he asked. Juliet hadn't been at the museum the night of the robbery, but Riley wasn't ready to dismiss anyone yet. "I wasn't able to interview her today. She had a scheduled vacation, starting today."

"The identity she used at the museum isn't valid. Juliet Manet didn't exist before two years ago. Her apartment's been searched. We don't know how deep the conspiracy went at the museum," Beck said, "but it's likely more than one person was involved. Either Emery knew something and died because of it, or he was involved himself. We don't have any leads on Juliet Manet yet. We found travel documents in her apartment for Bermuda. We're working to verify now."

Riley's gut tightened. "What do you know about Richard Avano? Any chance he was involved?" And was there any chance he just loathed Avano for looking at Nina as if she were *his* to protect? No wonder the police and PAX didn't trust his instincts on this case.

"Avano's disappeared. Possibly fled the country. We know he took his passport. We're checking air and rail lines now.

"We made contact with the El Zarpan ambassador," Beck continued. "The ambassador needed a little coercion, but he admitted it was Avano who brought the idea to him of the stones being a hoax. In the ambassador's opinion, there was some competition or jealousy behind it, but the government of El Zarpa already regretted letting the stones leave the country and they were eager to pursue it."

Riley didn't like the possibility that the whole matter could be put down to an envious museum director. And the maze of people who were suddenly dead or disappearing left him with a rising sense of urgency. This wasn't about the museum. The stones were the key.

"My visions—"

"—could easily be skewed on this subject," Beck reminded him. "We're continuing to pursue all possibilities, but we can't place the entire agency's resources in one basket. We've got agents in Peru on the hunt for Cristobal's base, and they're looking for the native, but we've been unable to locate him. It's highly likely in his case that he's gone underground due to pressure from the government."

That was possible, but Riley still didn't buy for a minute that Avano was the endgame on this situation, though he could see how Beck would have his doubts. He had no evidence that Nina was the center of a terrorist plot, and there was plenty to suggest otherwise.

"What about the locksmith?" he asked. "Either he was paid off, or he was replaced with someone who wanted access to Dr. Phillips' apartment."

"He hasn't turned up. We don't have information on him. Dr. Phillips' apartment appears on his manifest for a work order today."

"Has he been reported as missing?"

"He's an alcoholic. He's known to take off on binges. We should have more information tomorrow. We've put a task force in place. Stay in touch."

Riley punched off, frustration gnawing through him. No matter what was going on, Nina was in danger.

The memory of how soft and perfect she'd felt in his arms crept unbidden into his mind, scorching him. He laced his hands behind his head and tried to turn off his brain. Outside, it was still raining, though the storm's ferocity had lessened. He could see rain sliding down the glass of the windows. And with every beat of his heart, he knew he was still as much of a coward as he'd been before he'd walked into that bedroom and told Nina he wanted her. It was more than desire. He still had feelings for her. It was that plain, and that awful.

"I thought of something."

He looked up and saw Nina standing there in the dark, innocent and beautiful and in so much more trouble than she realized. There were no tears on her cheeks, as he might have expected after their last conversation. There was just a weariness that was somehow more disturbing.

"It's what they're holding in their hands," she said quietly.

He sat up, not comprehending what she was getting at, but she looked so intense standing there, the baggy sleep shirt she wore falling around her hips. Her legs and feet were bare and he ached for nothing more than to take her into his arms again.

"The men in the robes," she went on, urgency filling her voice. "There's one on each stone, and they're holding something up—it looks like a stone. At least, that's what I think they're holding up. I hadn't really thought of it before. They're kind of just the background, you know? I was more interested in the main depiction on each stone. The medical miracles, the dinosaurs, the ancient spacecraft. But I was just thinking about the electromagnetic forces."

He sat up. She'd moved to the computer and pressed the button to turn it back on.

"I don't know your password," she said, lifting eyes to him that were alight with enthusiasm.

He crossed the room without switching on the light, leaned over her where she'd sat on the cushioned folding chair again, and typed in his password. The intoxicating sexy-clean swirl of her hit him.

The screen lit and she clicked on the program that would let her onto the Internet. He pulled up the other chair.

He watched her link quickly to a map of Peru. She

copied it and clicked through to the file with the combination of digital images of the stones they'd created earlier. She pulled the map into the center of the screen, then minimized the images of the stones, pulling them back and forth, clicking so fast his eyes had trouble keeping up.

"The lines of magnetic flux are most concentrated in the highest altitudes," she said softly, intent on her task, not away from the screen for a beat. "At least, that's what the ancients believed."

She aligned and realigned the stones, two by two, down the range of Andean mountains. The robe-clad men in the background of each stone were unevenly distributed, each stone entirely unique.

"I just thought—what if the stones in their hands could somehow be lined up in accordance with the geographical peaks. Then that would make sense with what the ancients believed about the power of the cosmos and the density of the magnetic flux."

She found two that fit, and shuffled the others. They fell into place, one after another clicking into direct line with the highest peaks.

"Oh my God," she breathed. .

Riley stared at the screen, transfixed. Eleven images marched, two by two, down the range, matching the peaks perfectly by the location of the outstretched hand with a stone. Covering every peak but one.

Hot prickling energy swept over him. *He saw the*

hand aligning the stones, reaching up to the heavens, invoking the ancients. The ocean rose up, swells beyond all belief hurtling floodwaters toward an innocent continent—

"They fit!" she cried, and he jerked from the vision outside his body to Nina's huge eyes. Shaken, cold, he struggled to focus and as he did, he made the next connection at the same time she did. "There's a stone missing. There should be twelve. You can see it now."

The certainty of her statement momentarily washed relief through him. If a stone was missing, then there was no way Cristobal could put them together, unleash whatever evil he intended.

But the relief was quickly followed by something icy grabbing hold of his gut.

"I didn't have much time the day I found them," Nina was saying. He could hear the frustration in her voice now, the realization that her find hadn't been complete. She didn't know, didn't understand, the vast horror that the missing stone could represent. "The El Zarpan government gave me one day. The native took me there, and—"

"Who knows where the stones were found?" Riley demanded.

Nina gazed up at him, and he could see something in his voice had frightened her. He didn't have time to offer comfort.

"The general area? El Zarpa isn't that large, of course," she explained slowly. "Everyone knows that's where I found them. But the majority of the island is made up of thick jungle. The natives are terrified of most of it because of the legends of the dark shamans. Supposedly they put a curse on the jungle and any who enter its heart will die a brutal death at the hands of a guardian beast. The El Zarpan people are poor and uneducated. Octavio, the native guide who took me there, said he'd seen the stones when he was a boy. He'd gotten lost from his family once and—"

"Octavio is missing," Riley interrupted her. "And so is Avano. Latest intel is that Avano is the one who prompted the hoax charges through the El Zarpan ambassador. There's a chance he's left the country now. Did Avano know where you found the stones? I mean, exactly."

Nina gasped. "Yes. Of course. He's the museum director. He was responsible for the project." She shook her head in disbelief. "He's the one who took this story to the ambassador?" Anger and hurt mixed in her voice. "Before he agreed to underwrite the expedition, I had to tell him where I believed the stones to be. I had a map, the one that Octavio made for me, and I showed it to Dr. Avano. It was in the papers that were stolen from my office. But it didn't show the location of the caves. I had to find them once I got there. Octavio knew where one of them was. I found the others."

She licked her lips, chewed on the soft bottom one. "Maybe it's a huge coincidence that they fit this way, but if I'm right, then anyone crazy enough to think they can harness some cosmic power with the stones would take them to the mountains. It's the magnetic lines, that's all. Could be anywhere along the grid."

Anywhere along the grid wasn't good enough. Not if Cristobol found the missing stone. All Cristobal had to do was come to the same conclusion Nina had and if the legends were true—

"You'll tell whoever you work for," Nina went on, hope flaring in her eyes. "They'll send men to find him—you know where to look. You'll get your terrorist, and I'll get the stones back. I know it'll take time but—"

"We don't have time."

Dozens of visions hit him at once, hurling him into space and time. Jumbled images of disasters, fires, floods, sounds of screams—

"Riley?"

"We don't have time." The words came out thick, urgent, his blood running ice-cold.

He realized Nina's hands were on his shoulders, her eyes terrified. "What is going on?" she whispered starkly. "Where do you go when you do that, when you look like that? It's like one second you're here, and the next you're not—but you are at the same time. You're scaring me. It's how you looked— Oh my God. It's how you looked in the hospital. Like your eyes were dead."

She dropped her hold on his shoulders and stumbled out of the chair. "What happened to you when you had that accident?"

He didn't want to tell her anything, but the power of the visions when he saw the stones aligned changed everything. Cristobal already had eleven of the stones. The magnetic grid would be a logical leap. He was studying the stones just as Nina had been. And Avano was missing.

The twelfth stone was all he needed and untold cataclysmic disasters could be unleashed on the Earth.

"I see things," he said, his voice low and hard, barely controlled. The force of the visions held him, the stones glowing from the screen in their deadly alignment.

Nina backed away from him as he stood, bumped against the counter that crossed into the tiny, dark kitchen.

"See what things?" Her voice came out small, shaky.

"The power of the stones is real," he told her. He was afraid to move toward her, afraid she'd scream.

He'd hidden himself away from intimate contact since the accident. The operation that had saved his life but filled his head with a connection to the world's worst evil. He'd convinced himself he was helping mankind, that his mission meant something, gave his life a meaning it had never had before. He'd walked among normal people as he'd continued his role in the police department, but he'd set himself apart.

Nina had pulled him close, opened his closed heart to human feelings again. And now she was looking at him as if he were a monster. The look in her eyes was crushing him, but if it was for the best, if it meant she'd finally understand the truth of why there was no future for them, then—

"I had an operation after the accident," he said, and the anger unleashed in his own voice stunned him. It had been against his will, this implantation of the sensor that connected him to evil. He hadn't realized his anger until now. "It saved my life. *They* saved my life."

"They? This secret agency you're working for?" She didn't move, didn't blink. Her slender body was held tensely, poised as if to run if need be. She was scared of him.

He had to go on. He had no choice now. "I explained to you that it's dangerous, this work I do." He'd gained the power to save the world, but lost the hope for his own heart. "It's important. It can save lives. Thousands, maybe hundreds of thousands of lives."

"What are these things that you see?"

"Evil in its purest form. Terrorism. I have the ability to foresee terror before it strikes."

He saw her throat move. The glow of the laptop screen lit the strained lines of her face.

"You knew in the museum that the stones had power," she guessed, crossing her arms around herself as if she were afraid her knees would buckle if she didn't hold herself up. "You knew something was wrong in my apartment last night." She trembled as she stood. "That's why you believed in me."

"I would have known anyway that you weren't involved in this crime, Nina," he said. If there was one true thing in this whole mess, it was that he believed in her.

"You said there's no time," she said, watching him warily. "You're afraid they'll find the other stone. And your—people, whoever they are—won't have time to find them before they use them. They may be able to use them anywhere along the magnetic grid. That's thousands of miles. And they're real. You— You see things that tell you they're real. Oh God, I found them." Horror filled her eyes. "If something terrible happens, it's my fault."

"No." The word burst out of him and without realizing it, he closed the final steps between them, gripped her trembling shoulders. "It's not your fault. You couldn't have known."

But she wasn't comforted. "Dr. Avano is missing." She repeated his earlier words, as if putting it all together in her mind. Her pained gaze lifted to his again. "If he was involved—" There was a hitch in her voice. She gained control and went on. "Whoever took those papers out of my office, whether it was Dr. Avano or someone else, has that map. If there's a stone still there, one I missed in the caves, and if he finds it and gives it to these terrorists—"

"We're not going to let that happen," he told her fiercely. "I need you to tell me where you found the stones."

She drew in a sharp breath. "You won't find it without the map, and even the map doesn't pinpoint the exact location of the caves."

"I have to take the chance. You can draw me another map. Mark the caves as best as you can."

"I won't," she said stubbornly even as she felt fragile in his arms. "I know where the stones were found. There were four caves, and I found four stones in three of them. In the last one, I only found three. That's where the last stone must be. I can find that cave again. I'm not sending you off with a half-assed map to your death."

He wanted to shake her. "I can't risk your life, Nina."

"But you can risk yours?"

"I'm a trained agent. I'll make it."

"You don't know that," she charged angrily. "You're still human, aren't you?"

He felt the prick of hot emotion. The desperate pull of her, too near, too strong. Her determined gaze locked with his, wouldn't let go. He was all too aware of the rush of need that penetrated even this urgent moment.

"Yes," he said roughly. "I'm still human."

The taut beat stretched unbearably between them.

"Then we'll do this together. We'll have this agency of yours behind us, right? I know they probably think I can't be trusted, but surely they'll want to follow this up. Surely they wouldn't take the risk of *not* following it up. I'm sure you've told them what you've seen—" She gasped. "It's not just me they don't trust, is it? But you're their—"

"Experiment," he finished for her. She stared at him, eyes wide and wet and desperate. "My visions could be skewed by— They know we have a past, Nina. I could be wrong about everything, and if this is a case of jealousy— It could simply be Avano setting you up, trying to hurt your reputation. Maybe he wants to play hero and find the last stone if he's somehow figured out that there's another one. Or maybe he has some other plan to authenticate the stones, some other angle for playing the hero and saving the museum, diminishing your role in the discovery."

"That's crazy."

Riley stared at her. "How well do you know Avano? Would you have believed that he would be the one who planted the hoax idea with the El Zarpan ambassador?"

Nina swallowed hard.

"Emery's death wasn't a suicide," Riley went on. "He was murdered, Nina. The locksmith who was scheduled to change your locks has disappeared. So has Juliet Manet."

"She's on vacation. She's had this planned for a long time—"

"Juliet Manet isn't her real name."

Nina's eyes went wide. "But the museum does background checks before—"

"Not good enough."

Nina was silent for a beat. "She told me once she'd had a terrible relationship with a former boyfriend. He stalked her, and I know she was terrified of him. Danny was always especially careful of walking her out because she was scared he would find her again. Maybe that's why she changed her name. I mean, I can't imagine Juliet's involved in any of this."

"Maybe she is, maybe she's not. Anything's possible at this point." He could see Nina was having a hard time digesting all the secrets and lies that had surrounded her at the museum. Her whole world had been turned upside down, and the truth was still unknown. "I could be wrong in what I believe is happening, Nina. Completely wrong. This could be a wild goose chase, thinking terrorists are involved. It could be nothing more than Avano's jealousy over your rise to prominence after you found the stones, but I don't think so. What we need is proof. My agency is on the case, but they aren't going to throw every resource out there on it without some evidence. I don't have any evidence, Nina. I only have what I believe."

He was in this thing on his own, and she had to know that.

Nina's gaze didn't shift. Impatience shimmered around her. "If you say this is what you see, then I believe you. And I'm not going to let you go alone. You have something to prove. Well, so do I. This is my life, my career. And you're going to have to take me because I won't tell you how to find them."

Anger and pain surged inside him. Sweet God, he didn't want this to happen. He didn't want Nina walking into danger by his side. At the same time, he admired the strong spirit inside her.

"Nina—"

"We don't have time to argue. We need to check flights. I'll need to make a list of gear we'll need, and

I'll need to pick up my passport back at the apartment."

She was already pushing past him, sitting down at the computer, tapping her way to an airline home page.

And she was right. He didn't have time to fight with her. And he didn't have time to even think about what it meant that she still trusted him this much.

Chapter 11

The first flight wouldn't be leaving until 7:00 a.m. Sleep was impossible. Everything Riley had told her shot around in Nina's mind. It all sounded so unbelievable, but he believed it. And he believed in her. The least she could do was return that faith.

She felt as if she'd stepped into an episode of *The Twilight Zone,* and the only way out was to find that last stone. She could be wrong. Riley thought he could be wrong. If they were both wrong, then nothing would be lost but the stones.

But if they were both right, the consequences could be enormous if they failed to act. And all she knew was that wherever Riley went, she was going, too. Even if he'd shocked her, he was her rock in a world that kept shifting under her feet. Even when he scared her, he made her feel safe.

It was five-thirty. The first weak light was breaking through the night-shrouded sky outside his apartment when he told her to get her things together. They stopped by her apartment, and he walked her to the door, didn't leave her side for a second while she retrieved her passport and gear. Then they headed to the airport.

They left his car in the short-term lot. She felt his hand firmly on her arm as they entered the terminal. The line at Peru Air was thankfully short in the wee hours of dawn. He requested tickets on the first flight to Arequipa, and made arrangements on a charter island carrier for the connection to El Zarpa.

Passengers lined up behind them as the terminal grew busier in the growing morning. Unnerved by even the thin crowd, Nina stepped closer to Riley. He wore another pair of worn jeans and a plain black T-shirt that made his shoulders look a mile wide and strong enough to hold up the world.

Riley slid his arm around her shoulders, tugged her close. She lifted her eyes to him and he smiled down at her. His hidden dimples winked. She remembered how he'd smiled at her that first night when they'd sneaked out of that charity event together like two kids cutting class.

His smile was wicked, warm and toe-curling.

She swallowed thickly over a lump that appeared instantly in her throat. He was faking it, making them blend in with the crowd of travelers. He knew she was nervous, worried about her unwelcome notoriety. Or was he concerned someone could be following them?

Goose bumps rose on her flesh, whether from Riley's nearness or the prospect of someone following them, she wasn't sure. Both were scary.

Tickets finally in hand, they left the airline counter and headed straight for security. Riley stopped, said something low to the man at the security station and before she knew it, he was being whisked to a room just off the security checkpoint.

"Don't move," he told her darkly.

When he came back, all she knew was that whatever he'd done inside that room meant he was able to cross through security with his gun holstered, concealed inside his jacket.

Keeping his stride even, they passed through to the gates. The smile was gone, replaced by a dark, edgy, dangerous air as his piercing gaze scanned the waiting passengers outside the gates. He held her hand, and she felt the commanding heat of him.

"That's our gate," she said, tugging his hand as he kept right on going, pulling her with him.

"Not yet."

Two gates down from the flight to Arequipa, he drew down the seat next to him as he settled in. "No tipping our hand," he said in her ear. "Just in case." The gate area was full where they'd stopped.

"Oh." He didn't want anyone to know they were headed for Peru. "I have to learn to think like a secret agent."

One side of his mouth quirked in a smile that touched her as sad. "Think like you're my girlfriend," he said in his bone-melting voice. "I'll think like a secret agent."

He slung his arm around the back of her seat, idly sliding his hand beneath her hair, brushing the back of her neck. Tingly warmth swept down her spine. *Think like you're my girlfriend.* Right. No problem. She could just pull that little dream out of the corner pocket of her heart where she'd put it thirteen months ago. One perfect fantasy, slightly used, minimal damage.

Still she gladly melted into his muscular shoulder. He was hard, tense, and she knew every fiber of his being was on the alert. She felt surrounded by him, his strength, his take-charge power, and the stark, demanding need inside her knew relief.

A middle-aged couple settled in across from them with an impossible measure of carry-on baggage. The wife opened a bottle of water, then ripped the top off a bag of cookies. She took a bite, watching Riley's leanly muscled form appreciatively.

Nina peeked a glance up at him, a ridiculously possessive streak heating her veins. He wasn't paying any attention to the woman ogling him. He was mouthwateringly good-looking, and she resisted the urge to tease him that there was no way he could get away with this secret agent stuff when he was so hot.

Seemingly idly, he stroked her hair, then tucked a wayward strand behind her ear. His fingers traced her jaw. He was watching the passengers straggling by in the terminal, not even looking at her, but she couldn't breathe when his fingers danced down her throat. Before he could look at her and see the heat that surely had to be in her eyes, she turned her cheek into his shoulder.

He stirred, just enough for his thigh to brush hers, and she resisted the urge to climb into his lap. What was wrong with her?

Brain drain. That was what happened to her when she got this close to Riley. All her life, people had praised her innate ability to focus, her determination to accomplish any task set before her. She'd learned early on that achievement was the one sure way to get her parents' attention. Her father was a driven politician, and her mother was an equally driven politician's wife, and their only child was the dot on their *i* that completed perfect family campaign ads. Nina hated everything about politics—the phoniness, the kissing up, the eternal quest for empty favor. She hated the falseness of her home where her parents treated each other in ice-cold fashion until, boom, the lights were on and the public was watching.

Riley was real. He'd never played games with her feelings, and maybe that's why she'd been so shocked when things had ended so abruptly.

And now she knew the bizarre truth about his accident. She still hadn't figured out what to do with it. He saw no future for them, and that he wanted her, desired her, didn't change anything. He'd made that quite plain.

If she started imagining anything different, she'd be crazy. But with his fingers still stroking her neck, her stomach quivering in response, there was no doubt that her famed focus was out of whack. Or maybe she was thinking about climbing into Riley's lap to keep herself from thinking about what was going to happen once they got to Arequipa.

"You holding up?" he whispered, his voice terrifyingly tender and low.

She lifted her head. "Sure."

"Do you need to call anyone? This is your last chance." A pay phone booth stood near the gate.

She shook her head. She'd left her cell phone back at her apartment, knowing it was useless to bring to South America. "My parents are still out of town, and even if they weren't…" She chewed her lip, looked down at her feet. "You know we're not that close. And since all this happened, with the hoax charges, things have been pretty tense."

"I'm sorry." His low voice brought her eyes back to him. His gaze had a compassionate intensity that made her want to cry. But then something changed in his eyes. He was looking beyond her now. She started to turn, but his hand moved, cupped the back of her head, drawing her back to him. Then she wasn't aware of anything else because his mouth was on hers.

It was a slow, deep, lazy kiss, as if he wanted to make it last, and she would have surrendered her soul to make it go on forever. Everything quickened inside her and she forgot they were in the terminal. Forgot they were headed for South America. Forgot they could be in danger.

Her senses unraveled with startling speed. A flood of arousal washed her away.

But forever wasn't in the cards.

He drew back slowly, his eyes tight on hers, full of passion and hunger that told her he hadn't wanted it to end, either.

If her heart were beating any harder, it would burst out of her chest. Her whole body felt weak, as if she were one big rag doll.

"Do you see that, dear?"

The voice tore her out of the magic hold of his

eyes. She twisted, saw the middle-aged woman across from them watching with an envious expression.

"I remember when you used to kiss me like that." She poked her husband then stuffed another cookie into her mouth.

Nina swallowed thickly, looked at Riley.

"Reporters at five o'clock," he whispered against her forehead, tucking her close again. "I'm sure they're just headed out on an assignment, but they could recognize you, want a story."

Peeking over his shoulder, she spotted a couple of men with camera equipment at the gate counter, arguing with the airline representative about something.

"Let's go get some breakfast before the flight, honey." His voice was rough, unbearably sexy. Riley rose and reached for her hand to pull her to her feet. He was getting her out of there before the reporters laid eyes on her.

Her knees wobbled as she took his hand and they walked away from the gate. That kiss had been a ploy, that's all. She looked up at him as he quickened their pace away from the gate.

His dangerous, hot gaze locked with hers. "I'm going to take care of you, Nina. I promise."

Even though they were among a growing crowd in the terminal as the morning wore on, they could have been alone. Just looking at him made her heart contract, her nerve ends jitter, and something way down low go pitter-patter.

"Just don't forget to take care of yourself," she said softly.

He didn't say anything.

The plane was packed. Riley ushered Nina into the window seat while he took the one on the aisle. They'd been among the last to board. As far as Riley could tell, no one suspicious had gotten aboard their flight. He'd meant his promise to Nina, but wondering how he was going to fulfill it would keep him from sleeping through the ten-hour trip no matter how exhausted he was at the moment.

Nina's profile was fragile as she stared out the window. She wore blue, her simple shirt outlining her soft curves. Jeans rode down her slender hips. Tough hiking boots, stained and scuffed from previous expeditions, fit her feet. She was ready.

Without looking at him, she reached blindly for his hand as the plane pulled away from the gate. Her fingers felt cold, but strong. *She* was strong, and completely amazing. He'd told her enough last night to send most women screaming for the hills. And yet she'd insisted on taking this trip with him, insisted on believing in him even when he wasn't sure he was right. She hadn't hesitated a beat before throwing caution to the winds and attempting to save the world right along with him, as if she did it every day.

He didn't want it to mean so much to him. He didn't want to need her. Two days ago, he could have sworn he didn't need anyone. But he needed her, more than he wanted to think about. That honeymoon act in the terminal had been no act, and those reporters had been nothing but a flimsy excuse.

The plane's engines throbbed as they picked up speed. A matching tension filled his chest, and his jaw tightened painfully.

Nina's face turned and her eyes caught his. She'd left her hair loose today and it settled around her face, framing it with a copper cloud.

"Are you okay?"

"Fine. Why?"

She cocked her head. "You're squeezing my hand off."

"Sorry." He let go of her hand. His palms were sweating. He made a point of not looking out the window as they lifted off. El Zarpa be damned, he just hoped he didn't throw up before they got there.

"You're scared of flying."

He stared at Nina. Her eyes, shatteringly nervous a moment before, danced curiously.

"I just don't like takeoffs." Or landings. Or the part in between. "Don't laugh."

She bit her bottom lip then, dammit, she laughed.

"That's so sweet," she said, her voice low and slightly choked, as if she were trying to stifle a laugh. "Big, bad superagent that you are and all."

"Stop it. It's not funny. It's—" Embarrassing. He was tough. He was a cop, not to mention a PAX agent. He could bench-press two-eighty.

"I think it's sexy," she said.

"I didn't grow up jet-setting like some people."

"Flying is far more safe than getting into your car," she pointed out.

"Unless you crash. Car crash—you might live. Plane crashes... People usually just have one of those."

She stared at him for a long beat. It had taken only one car accident to destroy what they'd had. He didn't know what to say, or if he should, or could, say anything.

"Look—" she said, breaking the moment, nodding at the window "—we're in the air."

And they were.

They changed planes in Houston. Their next flight was delayed due to the stormy weather that seemed to have followed them all the way from Washington, D.C. After an excruciating two-hour layover, they were on their way to Arequipa.

"Take a nap," Riley urged her as they settled in for the second leg of the journey.

"What if you get scared all alone?" Was she flirting or teasing? The whole endearing thing about him being afraid to fly made her want to kiss him. *Bad Nina. Go to sleep.*

"I'll be fine."

"I bet you were a cute little boy." Had her mouth run off with her tongue?

"I was a brat. You wouldn't have liked me."

She leaned her head back against the seat. "Maybe someday you can tell me all about it." Like now. She wished he'd keep talking.

A muscle jumped in his hard jaw. "Nothing to tell."

That's the line he'd always given her when it came to his past. "I bet there is."

He didn't say anything.

"Come on, tell me a bedtime story," she said softly.

"Then I'd have to make it up," he said, his look dry.

"No more lies, remember?"

He fell silent again and she thought he wasn't going to tell her anything at all, but then he spoke and she had to lean toward him to hear him over the hum of the plane.

"I don't remember how long I was in the house by myself," he said. "I was eight. I ate everything in the cupboards and the fridge. I was down to a half box of crackers. Is this maudlin enough yet?"

Hurt filled her chest. "I just want to know the truth."

Whether he wanted to admit it or not, he had some pretty angry feelings about this past of his that he never talked about. She knew he hadn't meant to take those feelings out on her.

"I know." He looked away. "The electricity had gone off a few days before, I remember that. I hated it when it got dark. The lady's name was Miriam Walters, I remember that, too. She worked for the state. She just showed up one day and took me away."

Nina couldn't keep quiet. "Where were your parents?"

"I don't know. My dad was a drunk, in and out of jail. I have no idea what became of him. My mother was on welfare, and she'd hooked up with some guy and taken off."

He was right—his was no bedtime story. It made her feel for him. "And your mother just left you there in the house by yourself?"

There was a bitter light in his gaze. "Her new boyfriend didn't like kids. Trust me, I wasn't sorry when he was gone."

"Did he…" She struggled to ask the question. "Did he hurt you?"

The lean lines of his face were unmoving. "You have to love someone for them to really hurt you, Nina."

Oh God. He *had* been hurt. Not just emotionally, but physically. She thought of how they'd met, both of them involved with an abused children's charity. She'd been on the board because her mother had arranged it. Riley had been representing the police department, but she knew he'd chosen to take the opportunity.

"So that's how you ended up at the boys' ranch?" She'd known before that he'd grown up on a Texas boys' ranch, but he'd never told her the full story.

"I told you, I was a brat. Not real adoptable."

Nobody'd wanted him. Her heart tightened.

"I liked the ranch," he went on, as if he'd forgotten she was there. "It was a working cattle ranch. I was there longer than most of the kids, so I got more responsibility. I was on my own a lot. Learned to rely on myself."

And not on others. He'd learned from the get-go, in the most painful way possible, that needing anyone led to heartache, she thought.

"How'd you wind up in D.C.?"

His expression was like granite. "Chance," he said. "I stayed on at the ranch after I turned eighteen. They paid me after I came of age. Earned enough money to buy a car that looked like it had been to hell and back. I got a two-year degree at the community college. When I was done with that, I closed my eyes, stabbed my finger at the map and took off."

"Anywhere but there?"

"There was nothing holding me there. I wanted a

fresh start. Found out when I got to D.C. that roping cattle wasn't a skill in high demand in the nation's capital." He met her gaze again. "But I was also an expert marksman. All those summer afternoons shooting cans behind the barn were good for something. I applied to the police academy."

"And now you're protecting the innocent." She watched him.

He reached over with his other hand, stroked the line of her jaw. "Trying to."

She spoke in a disgusted burst. "No wonder I seemed like such a spoiled princess to you, with my trust fund and my fancy apartment and my flashy parents."

"Money doesn't buy happiness," he reminded her, and the tender sadness in his eyes was more intimate than a kiss. "Or even mean a hell of a lot about a person. I don't like to admit this ordinarily, but I used to be stupid."

He was telling her he'd let his pride stand in the way in the past when it came to her money. That he might not let that happen now didn't make her feel the least bit better. His desire for her was clearly written in his eyes.

They were headed straight into a life-and-death situation, and the future was just as fraught with emotional peril.

"You're smarter now?" she asked.

His lips quirked. “Not much.” His dark-rimmed blue eyes were pinned on the horizon outside the plane. “Not much.”

Chapter 12

He was, in fact, downright dumb, Riley decided when they arrived in El Zarpa. He had no idea what time it was, and standing outside the dirt runway in the moisture-rich island night, waiting for the car they'd rented, it was too dark to care. They were both worn to the bone and the trip from hell had only just begun. Worry was eating him away. He wished to God Nina was back in D.C.

"I could eat a horse," she said, pushing damp tendrils out of her pale face. "Make that three." Her weary smile was the sexiest thing he'd ever seen. "Sorry. I guess I shouldn't talk that way to a cowboy." Another slow beat slid. "You sure made something of yourself, Riley Tremaine."

He felt a tug deep inside at the long look she gave him. There was respect, and something else. Sympathy, maybe. What had made him tell her all that about his nasty childhood trauma? He'd gone all of his adult life without talking about it out loud. The wounds were there, but he had buried them deep.

He'd given a piece of himself to Nina now that he hadn't given anyone else. It bothered him, the way she slid into his skin and got him to open up.

A vehicle pulled up from the dim recesses of the rental car lot behind the airport terminal building that looked suspiciously like a big barn, which he supposed matched the tiny plane they'd chartered from Arequipa. It had resembled a tractor with wings. The car rattled and smoked, but it ran.

Nina slid in on the passenger side. Riley took the wheel. The attendant handed Riley a crumpled map and took off. Nina took it out of his hands.

"I know the way," she said, pointing right when they came out the dirt drive to the only slightly more respectable road to Los Mitos. Even in the dark, the El Zarpan town revealed its poverty in the low-slung outlying shacks, almost piled atop each other on the cascading shadowed streets. The dark road opened up suddenly to a more respectable-looking, palm-lined avenue with small shops, a closed bazaar, then moon-washed government buildings made of white volcanic rock. The ocean shimmered to one side and several miles farther, a sprawling, aging resort appeared.

"They don't have much tourist business now," Nina said. "We won't have any trouble getting a room." They hadn't had time to call in advance. "It was nearly empty every time I was here. El Zarpa used to attract adventure travelers, but there's been a lot of political instability in the past decade. Even though things are calmer now, the tourists haven't come back."

Riley parked in front of the hotel office. "Would the hotel staff recognize you then, remember you?"

She bit her lip, nodded. "I think they might."

Terrorists weren't the only issue in El Zarpa. Nina no longer had the government's sanction to search for or remove artifacts. They'd cross that bridge when they came to it. PAX had ways. But for now, he didn't need government officials breathing down their necks. There was already a chance that Nina's name would be spotted as having come through customs at the airport. No point in increasing her visibility here.

"Then sit tight."

The lobby was floored in colorful ceramic tiles and adorned with flamboyant plants boasting leaves broader than his chest. Growing up in Texas, he had a working knowledge of Spanish and managed to get the point across to the tiny, dark old a man who sat behind the lobby desk listening to salsa music on a tinny-sounding radio. The attendant scrawled a circle on a photocopied map of the hotel property and pushed it across the scarred hardwood counter.

"Any other Americans check in tonight?" Riley asked him in Spanish. He wasn't sure what he was expecting to hear.

The man shook his head.

Riley returned to Nina and they drove around to the rear of the complex. The hotel was laid out in a rectangle, with a lush, tropical, kidney-shaped pool in the central courtyard. They had one of the rooms with a rear patio opening out onto the beach. Few of the rooms revealed any light at the windows. Occupancy was low.

Taking overnight necessities only, they left the car to head across the cobbled path that led into the courtyard. In the yellow glow of the lantern that swung from the side of the hotel room door, Riley opened the door. Nina looked ready to fall asleep on her feet, and he felt the same way.

When they stepped inside and flipped the switch that lit a lamp by the bed, he realized he had clearly misunderstood the attendant on one thing. The room had one king-size bed, not two double beds. The bed itself was swathed in romantically draped mosquito netting.

He shut the door. "Sorry," he said. "I thought we

were getting two beds. It's not safe for you to be in a room by yourself, but I can go back—"

"No, of course not." Nina's huge, exhausted eyes connected with his. "You're tired. Don't be silly." She dropped her things and sat on the end of the bed. Her shimmery copper hair tumbled around her head as she flopped backward. The blue cotton shirt she wore rode up, revealing her smooth bare stomach. Just watching her was fascinating. She was all graceful long limbs and smooth beautiful movements. "Let's just go to bed."

Apparently he wasn't tired enough to stop her innocently dropped *let's just go to bed* from affecting his nether regions.

She tipped her head to the side, watching him from beneath heavy lids. "We can be grown-up about this, can't we? You're not going to say something stupid like that you'll take the chair? Because those chairs over there don't look comfortable at all."

They didn't. There were two chairs, bamboo contraptions with mounds of brightly patterned pillows, and they were far too small for him to sleep in. They were set at a small glass table situated for an ocean view through the patio doors. The only other furniture in the room was a narrow dresser with a rather outdated television. But he wanted to touch Nina so badly, even worn out as he was, that he shook with the need. He had a whole host of memories of how it felt to run his hands along that satiny flesh….

"I'll just grab a blanket and some pillows and sleep on the floor," he offered.

"Well, okay, but they have scorpions here. When I was here last time, they were crawling all over the hotel room. It's bad enough walking around here. You don't want to sleep on this floor." She leaned up, watching him. "You don't need to worry about compromising my reputation, you know. I have no reputation left."

She was in danger, and he damned his body for having a whole different set of priorities from his brain. He was wrong to have brought her here at all, even if her help was essential to finding the stone. He wanted Nina to have a decent life, a safe life.

"Don't talk as if your life is over," he said sharply. "It's not."

She squeezed her eyes shut and turned away. But not before he saw the sheen of dampness. "You don't know that, and neither do I. No more lies, remember?" She opened her eyes, her gaze soft and haunted. "All I know is I'm glad there aren't two beds. I don't want to be alone tonight."

No more lies. She'd said that herself, and she'd never meant it more than she did now. They could die, both of them. Maybe even tomorrow.

He'd showered after she had, returning to the darkened room wearing faded jeans that hugged his lean, long legs and another T-shirt, untucked. He was barefoot, and his hair stuck wetly to his head. She sat in her own oversize sleep shirt, legs crossed under her, in the middle of the big bed with its mosquito net shroud, watching some kind of Spanish game show on TV. She should have been fast asleep, but nerves kept her awake. She watched him take a satellite phone out of his bag and place a call. He gave their location in Los Mitos and punched off. The fact that his secret agency knew where they were should have made her feel safer, but it only made her more aware of how little she knew about Riley despite what he'd told her today.

He crossed to the locked bar, leaned down and slid the hotel room key into the slot to open it. He pulled out two small bottles and a can.

She punched the remote to switch off the television, leaving the room bathed only in the low lamplight. The midnight view of the pool and the ocean was hidden by the draped curtains at the courtyard window and the beachfront patio.

"Rum and Coke?" He straightened and turned back to her.

"I don't want anything," she said. Even as tired as she was, her stomach was restless and her nerves jittery.

His eyes were distant, his face grim. She knew what he was doing. He was pushing her away, despite the intimacy of the setting, the desperation of the situation. And she'd meant what she said. She didn't want to be alone. She wanted arms around her. Riley's arms. She was too tired, too scared, too unhappy to worry about all the reasons why indulging in that need could be dangerous.

"The alcohol would help you sleep," he said.

The ache in her chest deepened. "That's not what I need."

"It's what I need." He twisted the cap on one of the bottles, poured it into a glass he took from the top of the dresser.

His back was to her now. Even through the T-shirt, she could see the rigid tension of his muscles. Quietly, she crossed the room to him. He smelled like hotel soap.

He didn't want to talk, she knew that. He wanted her to go to sleep. He didn't want to face what burned between them or that he couldn't promise everything was going to be okay.

Caution warned her to leave him alone. He was suffering his own torment. She could be angry and frustrated that he'd walked away from her because of his life as a secret agent and these visions he had, but he was the one who had to live that life and it couldn't be easy.

She was tired of caution. She didn't want to die without knowing Riley's touch one more time. Even if it was the last time. The possibility that she could end up hurt all over again didn't matter. She was *already* hurting.

Tonight, there was just the two of them, here in this hotel room, hidden away from the world and all the problems back in D.C., even the dangers waiting here on this island.

Her desperate need to touch him took over. He'd poured Coke into the glass with the rum and, with his head tipped back, he swallowed a long drink and turned. She held his starkly aching gaze.

"It's a fool who finds his courage in a bottle," she said softly.

His expression was tight. "I'm looking for sleep, not courage." He scraped his fingers through his wet hair. "I'm sorry I brought you here, Nina. I'm sorry all of this has happened and that you were at the center of it. I'm sorry you've been hurt, and I don't want to hurt you anymore."

"You think it doesn't hurt me to not have your arms around me right now?" Her voice broke just a little, and she took a ragged breath.

The utter devastation of his eyes gave her the strength to go on, hoping she was breaking through the darkness he cloaked himself in.

"It's possible neither one of us has a future," she

said. "And don't—" she spoke louder before he could deny it "—don't tell me I'm wrong."

His eyes burned with torment.

"But we're both alive tonight," she went on. "And I know you think this thing inside you, what happened to you after the accident, changed you, changed everything. But you were wrong."

His gaze now was intense and full of pain. She didn't hesitate, just reached up, took his face in her hands.

"It didn't change this," she breathed and then kissed him. She felt the shuddering reaction inside him, knew the heat of his response in the way his mouth pressed against hers. No matter how much he tried to deny it, the need was real.

"Stop this before it's too late." His voice was hoarse against her lips. "You don't know what you're doing to me. I'm an experiment, Nina. Remember that? Proceed with caution, because you shouldn't trust me. I don't even trust myself."

"I'm tired of caution." She twined her arms around his neck and brushed her mouth against his again. She could feel the hard ridge of him pressed against her body.

"Nina," he breathed against her mouth. "It's my job to take care of you."

"Stop taking care of me. And just care."

A hard sound emerged from deep in his throat.

Then his arms swooped around her, and together they tumbled back a few steps and fell onto the bed. His mouth was on her lips, her neck, her ears.

Hunger crashed in her veins. She didn't want to think. She wanted to cry, and she wanted to scream for him to hurry. She'd been waiting thirteen months for this moment, and she hadn't even known it until now.

His hand slid beneath her T-shirt, heating her cold skin. His face lifted to hers, a haunting question crossing his gaze.

"Nina—"

"Don't stop." She reached between them, pulled up to rip off the shirt, leaving herself bare except for the sensible cotton panties she wore. "I need you. Just need me back. Make love to me. Now."

He responded by claiming her mouth again, pressing her back against the soft piled pillows. In the shroud of the mosquito netting, the world fell away. There was nothing but his devouring mouth, his strong arms, his hard body and a need they shared that was no longer denied.

Fire tore through her veins as he left her mouth to murmur her name, husky and deep, and slide his tongue down her neck, to her chest, settling on one taut, aching nipple. Desire jolted through her, and she whimpered as he tugged with his mouth, his hand skimming lower, slipping between her thighs.

She arched against him, pressing her sensitive mound into his hand. She tore at his shirt, and he sat up long enough to pull it over his head. The powerful line of his shoulders shone in the shadowed light. She found the zipper of his jeans and tugged it down. With a groan, he rose and kicked them off, returning to her naked and hard, the wall of his control gone. The hunger radiating from him was thunderous and the anticipation of his wild demand left her weak.

She ached to know every inch of him, for him to know every inch of her. Urgency washed over her.

She reached for him, scraping her fingers through the springy mat of hair on his broad chest, sliding around his neck and then pulling him atop her. He tangled his hands in her hair, slammed his mouth over hers again.

The sensation of him against her stomach, the fury of his sweet kisses, left her dizzy and shaking. Her legs wrapped around him of their own accord, her hips tilted into him. His mouth never leaving hers, he rolled to the side, reaching between her thighs for the heat she tipped into his palm.

Her panties disappeared, slipped away under his desperate touch, and then his fingers stroked inside her. She all but fell apart right then and there. Her heart pounded, and blood thumped down her veins. Sinking her nails into his shoulders, she cried his name. He didn't stop and she didn't want him to, but he slid down, until his mouth trailed along her belly and his teeth bit her thigh. Then he kissed the screaming, needy folds between her legs and she fisted her fingers into the bedsheets, her senses spinning wildly as he sucked. His name broke from her mouth time and again.

Her body remembered every kiss, every touch, every suckling, delirious pressure. The combination of gentle and fierce ministrations was so familiar, so wonderful. She went ridiculously fast, over the edge, into an oblivion that she remembered too well.

He came back, sliding his lips over her torso, reaching her breasts again, then her neck, then her ear.

"I want to be inside you," he breathed. "I want you, Nina."

She reached him, guided him inside her. She wanted to feel him within her, his heat filling up all her empty places where she ached and burned for him.

She pushed against him and he drove into her, matching her arching rhythm. He ravaged her with his mouth, his lips, his teeth as he rocked again and again. The pleasure built so quickly, she could barely keep up with it.

Her senses flickered, and her heart exploded when he breathed her name brokenly against her mouth as she dug her fingers into his back. She'd proven her point. He wasn't unaffected, and that fact blew her away, blew away the fabric of her own fakery, the one lie she'd let go.

The lie that this was just one night and that tomorrow didn't matter. The lie that she didn't still love him.

But it was far too late now, and all she could do was hang on for dear life, shuddering wildly as his whole body tightened and he flew out of control right along with her. Nothing mattered but the man in her arms and the sensation of completeness she'd never known with anyone else.

She'd forgotten how giddy, how wonderful, it was to be in love. She'd been fighting it, fighting his memory, but he wasn't a memory anymore and she was all done fighting. She could feel him beside her now, breathing hard, still holding on to her. He needed her as much as she needed him. He'd shown her what he couldn't tell her, shown her in his hunger, his tenderness, his loss of control.

Surrender glided through her. She was in love with Riley Tremaine.

And he would just have to get used to it because this time, she wasn't going to make it easy for him to back away.

Chapter 13

Riley lay awake in the dawn-cloaked room. The softness of Nina's arm sleepily brushed against his side as she spooned into him.

"Make love to me again," she whispered sleepily, sexily. "I miss you already."

He wanted nothing more than to do exactly that. She shifted, moved, nibbled his earlobe. Her slender leg wrapped over his. He turned his head, found her gaze close in the shadows. Pain scorched him as he looked into her shining eyes.

Grief tightened his chest. He wanted to take her, hold her, make love to her. He wanted everything he knew he could never have. Most of all, he wanted to go back in time two days to when he hadn't remembered how much he wanted Nina.

He shoved back the feelings, closing his eyes against them, and opened them to find the confusion in Nina's gaze. He'd come close, so close, over a year ago to losing himself in her, to letting himself love her. The accident had changed everything, just in time. He'd broken it off with her and as painful as that had been, it had been a relief. He didn't want to love her. He didn't want to love anyone. Their relationship had gotten out of control.

Last night had gotten out of control.

He'd been so careful, and now—

Breath jammed suddenly, raw, in his throat. He hadn't been careful last night. *They* hadn't been careful.

"Riley?" she whispered.

"I shouldn't have let this happen." He sat up, grabbed his jeans from the floor and shoved one leg at a time into them, then turned. "And we can't let it happen again."

Nina blinked. Her body stiffened. "Can't let what happen?" She pushed herself up on one elbow. "Can't make love, or can't be honest? Because I think what happened last night is the most honest thing we've shared in a year, and if you're worried that I can't handle it, that I'll be hurt—"

She broke off, a bitter shake to her voice.

"We didn't use protection, Nina." He damned himself to hell for that lapse. He'd given in too easily last night to the fantasy of being with Nina. He'd resolved not to touch her, then he'd done the opposite. He'd resolved to protect her, then he'd put her in danger. He'd vowed not to feel anything, then he'd felt way too much.

All he had to do was look at her, and she splintered his soul. He needed his control back, desperately.

She sat now, dragging the sheet with her as if suddenly conscious of her nudity, even in the semidarkness.

"Don't you think we have bigger things to worry about?"

"No. No, I don't."

He could see the anger rise in her cheeks.

"Then I'm glad to know you think the possibility of having a baby with me is a fate worse than death."

God, he'd hurt her. But he couldn't give her what she needed, and pretending would only hurt her more. "Dammit, Nina, that's not what I'm saying."

In his mind, he kept seeing her over and over, opening herself to him, giving him all the sweetness and hope inside her. Giving him everything.

He had nothing to give back.

"Then what are you saying?" she demanded, her hot gaze pinned to him.

He went back to the bed, back to her. He sat, reached toward her, unbearably drawn to touch her. She didn't flinch when he skimmed his fingertips along her taut jaw, didn't back away. Her soft skin, her fierce eyes, intoxicated him.

"You're beautiful, Nina. Last night was beautiful. But it was wrong. And what I'm saying is you don't want to have my baby."

"Now you know what I want?"

He closed his eyes again, forced himself to drop his hand, to move away from her. "Nina, nobody should want to have my baby." He stood, reached for the shirt he'd tossed on the back of one of the bamboo chairs. "Even if we make it off this island and out of this situation alive, I'm not going to settle down with you and a white picket fence."

"Did I ask for a picket fence?"

He pulled the shirt over his head. She hadn't moved from the bed. "You will."

"Would you stop telling me what I want? Maybe I want to have a baby with you. Has that ever crossed your mind? I didn't plan for that to happen last night, but if a baby is the result, then it's not going to scare me. Do you see me having a panic attack this morning because we didn't use protection?"

No. She wasn't upset about it. She didn't seem scared at all. And that made his whole chest ache. It scared *him.* It scared him a lot.

"Why the hell would you want to have a baby with me?"

The words broke from her. "Did it ever cross your arrogant mind that I love you?"

No. No, no and no. "Nina—"

She pulled the sheet tighter around herself, but her eyes didn't waver. "I'm going to be honest, even if you can't—or won't—be. I love you. There." Chin tipped, she glared at him. "Deal with it, Tremaine."

She was calling him Tremaine. Not Riley. It was the bare slip of defensiveness that cracked his heart.

He stared at her, nearly blinded by the anguish in the room. "I can't deal with it." His voice came out raspy, strained. *I love you.* She had no idea how much he couldn't deal with that.

"Can't, or won't?"

He turned, strode across the room. "It doesn't matter."

Grabbing his shaving kit from the bathroom, he brought it out, stuffed it in his bag. The conversation was over. The fantasy of sleeping with Nina again was over. He was doing the right thing. He'd hurt her, but the buck stopped here. He wouldn't hurt her anymore.

He wouldn't lose control anymore.

She wasn't finished, though. "I think it does matter. I think it matters a lot. I think the big lie is the one you're telling yourself."

He didn't answer, just grabbed his boots and sat down on the end of the bed to put them on. "Get your things, Nina. We don't have time for this."

"You know, I may not be a detective, but I can see the clues. You got thrown off the case by the department—even they thought you weren't objective about me. I'd lay bets your secret agency doesn't think you're objective about me either, do they?"

He didn't answer.

That didn't stop her. "You believed in me when no one else did. You wanted to make love to me last night. I didn't exactly twist your arm."

"I'm a man, Nina. You offered. I took. Men do that."

"*You* don't do that."

Boots on, he stood and turned. She sat there still, in the bed where they'd made love.

"How do you know? Face it, Nina, you don't really know me. I'm a selfish son of a bitch."

"I know you better than you think. I might even know you better than you know yourself. I know that you think if you don't love someone, they can't hurt you. That's it, isn't it, Riley? I think this secret agency thing is a handy excuse. It's not what's really stopping you. But you're right about one thing. You *are* selfish. You're so damn selfish you'd rather leave me out on this limb all alone than risk facing the truth."

The taut silence stretched in the charged air. Something inside him twisted, slowly and deeply.

"I love you," she said again. "Why can't you accept that? Why can't you take what I'm giving you?"

She said it as if it were just that easy when he knew it wasn't. "Don't say that."

Abruptly, Nina rose off the bed, dropping the sheet. He knew it was deliberate, knew the pain in her eyes. She stood before him, naked and unafraid, the morning light creeping through the edges of the draped windows lighting her skin.

"Maybe you're right about one other thing." Hurt burned in her voice. "Maybe I don't want your baby. I wouldn't want my baby's father to be such a coward."

She grabbed her clothes from the floor and disappeared into the bathroom. The conversation was finally over. *They* were finally over.

Maybe he'd finally succeeded in making her hate him the way she should have hated him thirteen months ago. All he knew was that he hated himself.

I love you. She'd come right out and said it. Nothing about last night had entailed commitment, and she'd known that going in. She didn't blame him for that.

She blamed him for his lies. She'd known that he had his secrets. But secrets were one thing; lies were another. It had been different when she'd thought he'd ended their relationship because he didn't love her. That had hurt, badly. But to know that he did care about her and still couldn't see any hope for a future between the two of them? That was so much worse.

She'd been honest, and she wasn't sorry about it. She wasn't giving up, but she was so mad that she wasn't speaking to him. He'd shut her out, and she had no idea what to do about it. She had too much pride to beg.

Nina looked up from the map in her hand. The rental car chugged and coughed as it climbed into the El Zarpan jungle. Riley's grip on the wheel was fierce, focused.

The sexy lover of the night before was gone. He still wore the familiar tight-fitting jeans and the T-shirt that stretched across his chest and the bunched muscles of his upper arms. But this was the agent, the man she didn't know, the man accustomed to danger. The man who pretended he had no heart.

"That way." She pointed to the right as they came to a fork in the rutted gash of a road. Navigation had been the be-all and end-all of their conversation since they'd left the hotel. It had been a long, bitter, silent drive.

El Zarpa was nearly two hundred miles long and seventy-five miles wide. Los Mitos was the only town of any significance. The rest was jungle—

mostly mountainous—and only dotted with the occasional village.

The roads that wound south were crumbling in disrepair and, as Nina knew too well, eventually ended. The heart of the jungle, considered cursed by the natives, was navigable only on foot.

After the road split, it began narrowing quickly, the jungle stretching fingers of vines toward them as if to eat them whole. Minutes turned into an hour as they crept slower and slower until the road turned into little more than a path.

They had everything they needed for the day-long trek into the remote jungle—water, dried fruit, flashlights, a compass and a global positioning unit. Her boots were in her backpack that she'd tossed on the backseat.

"This is it," she said when he stopped, the car hemmed in almost completely now by the jungle. "It's as far as we can go by car."

She pushed open her door, unable to deny the sense of excitement that returned as memories of the initial discovery of the El Zarpa stones surged through her. It had all started here. Remorse and fear tangled inside her, too. If she'd never discovered the stones…

But it was too late for regret. And it was too late for regret about what had happened last night and this morning, too. Her heart turned over as she looked across the top of the car at Riley. He'd gotten out, and his gaze slowly turned from the dark jungle to her. A bird circled, then darted into the trees with a sharp cry.

She grabbed her backpack from the back of the car and sat down in the open door to tug on her boots. She tucked her jeans into the boots then put on a long-sleeved shirt over her lightweight tee to protect her arms. She went through the pack carefully, counting out each item, making sure they had everything they needed. The thought of getting lost scared her to death and she'd taken extra precautions on each expedition. Chemical lights, extra batteries, a mirror that could be used to catch the scant light deep inside the jungle to signal for help.

There wouldn't be any help waiting this time, though. No grad student assistants on call back at the car, watching and waiting. No nervous native leading the way.

Riley was on his satellite phone.

"There'll be a plane waiting for us at the airstrip tonight," he told her. He closed the phone, stuck it in his pack.

"Any news?"

"Still no word on Avano's whereabouts. Juliet Manet did check in to a resort in Bermuda." He watched her for a long beat in the still, damp air. "The locksmith was found dead this morning in his van. Bullet to the head."

Nina swallowed thickly.

"They had a man inside one of Cristobal's cells, but they've lost contact with him. They're getting closer to finding his camp. They've dispatched more agents, and hopefully it'll be soon enough for him and for us." With his gun holstered across his shoulder and back and clothed in his black T-shirt, he looked like one of the rebel soldiers that were once a common sight in the El Zarpan countryside. "Ready?"

She assumed the plane he'd mentioned had something to do with the secret agency of his. There was no way they'd get through customs with an illicitly obtained artifact.

But first they had to find it.

Nina slung her pack onto her back. "Ready as I'll ever be."

If the air on the beach in Los Mitos had been thick, it was nothing compared to stepping inside the jungle. The air there was so heavy that it was almost tangible, smothering them. Nina had a flashlight out already, directed at the compass in her hand, as they picked their way into a preternatural world that looked like something out of the age of dinosaurs.

She never lost her awe for the sheer magnitude of the surroundings. The trees were like skyscrapers, and it was almost as if you could see the umbrella-sized leaves of the vegetation growing right before your eyes. The canopy of branches cloaked the sky, leaving them to walk through a never-ending twilight filled with mysterious rustlings and skitterings.

Nina carefully trekked the path by memory, Riley's dark presence a source of strange comfort here despite the charged tension between them. While she'd never believed the natives' tales of the jungle being cursed, the eerie sense of being watched by a legendary beast, the shadowy remainder of the last shaman, never completely left her imagination.

If the stones were real, was the jaguar-like beast real, too?

Her pulse sped up, and she shook herself to focus. There were dangers in the jungle, real ones—snakes, spiders, a whole host of poisonous insects and plants. And the biggest danger of all—getting lost, like the man from the old plane whose skeleton she'd found in the last cave on her final expedition.

The last thing she wanted to do today was get lost. Three hours in, three hours out. It had taken them two hours just to get there. They had no time for trouble. She tried not to think about snakes and insects and terrorists who could be lurking anywhere. Leaves and vines brushed at them continually like greedy, grasping hands.

They were two and a half hours in when they hit a clearing where the sky tore through. A wrecked

Piper Cub lay in a tangle of metal and vines. Sun glinted off a broken wing.

"What the hell?" Riley stopped beside her, then moved past her, curious.

"I'm sure we're on the right track now," she told him. "The plane is my best marker."

He stared back at her. "It's pretty old."

"It's a Piper Cub, probably from the forties." She adjusted her pack, even the deliberately calculated light weight of it wearing on her muscles after this much time. They'd stopped once for water and a brief snack, but it had been months since she'd worked out this hard. "My father is an old plane buff," she explained.

"I wonder what happened." Riley leaned in to examine the plane's interior, what could be seen through the thick growth claiming it.

"I don't know what he was doing flying over this area," Nina said. "But I do know what happened to him."

Riley straightened, looked back at her. "How?"

"He got lost. I found a skeleton in one of the caves. He must have gone in circles trying to find his way out—an easy enough mistake to make when you can see so little sky for guidance. He probably took shelter there, and that's where he died. Possibly he'd been hurt somehow—either from the crash or in the jungle. The skull is damaged. I looked for identification, just out of curiosity, and didn't find any on him, at least none that hadn't disintegrated. I suspected from the remains of the clothing that he would have been the pilot."

If things went terribly wrong here—if the terrorists were here, in the jungle, now, and they found her and Riley—then someday someone else might find their remains in that cave.

"It's not far now," she told him.

Riley's eyes looked strange as he stepped toward her from the clearing, into the shadows where she stood. "Let's go."

She stared at the plane, then at Riley again. Her heart thumped. "What if we don't find the stone?" What if something *did* happen to them out here, the last thing between them would be that ugly scene this morning in the hotel. "Riley—"

His eyes were hollow, darkened. Dead.

"Riley?" Something awful rose in her throat.

He blinked, as if he'd been gone. "The stone is here," he said roughly. They stood there in the darkening shadows, the towering trees sighing above them. A bird called from far away. "How close are we to the cave?"

She swallowed hard. "Maybe another twenty, thirty minutes. Why? What's wrong?" What was he seeing? What wasn't he telling her?

His gaze burned her. "We're running out of time."

Chapter 14

Spray from the waterfall soaked them even as they ducked behind the monumental onrush of water pouring down from the cliff rising above them. There was no time to appreciate the beauty of the scene—the wide fall of white water into the deepest, bluest pool she'd ever seen, surrounded by the vibrant, unbroken green of jungle vegetation.

"Down here," Nina said, but the roar of the waterfall covered her voice. She used hand signals to show Riley the fissure tucked behind the cascading water, the crack of rock that looked like nothing more than a cubbyhole in the cliff.

She threw her pack down, and got on her hands

and knees to half crawl, half slide into the crevice. Once through, she leaned back to grab her pack.

Riley came through after her. Standing, Nina threw the glow of her flashlight around the large opening of the cave. The main chamber was deep and oblong. The air was damp and cold. Tree roots broke through the rock and protruded like eerie, grasping hands. To one side lay a passage that she knew from past experience led nowhere but to the pilot's skeleton.

"I searched for this cave for hours on that last day," she said quietly, her voice echoing eerily off the damp, dark walls. The sound of the waterfall came muted, distant, as if suddenly far away. "I wasn't even sure there was another one. But they were all in pretty close proximity, so I didn't want to leave without being sure." She looked around, feeling the strangeness of being back minus the excitement of that final expedition. "But I left without finding everything, after all."

The twelfth stone, if it existed, had to be here.

"Riley?"

In the shadow world of the cave, she moved her light, careful not to direct it straight into his eyes. He stood unmoving, and she saw that dead look in his eyes that terrified her.

Water. More water than he'd ever seen in his life. More water than could possibly exist roared toward him. Women screamed, children ran. A shadowy figure rose above the scene, replacing the shouts and the water. He was in a cave. Fire burned from his fingertips. The stone glowed and moved, out of the figure's hand, tore through the air—

Riley staggered backward, hit the wall of the cave.

"Riley!"

Someone was calling his name, shaking his shoulders. Then a gentle touch cupped his face. He was blind for an awful beat.

Then he saw Nina. She'd dropped the flashlight, but the scant glow hit her cheeks from where it lay on the ground. Her eyes sparked with worry.

"What's wrong?"

"The stone," he said thickly. He felt it, felt it as if it were pulling him. His skin tightened, his chest burned. "The stone is here."

Nina stared at him. "Help me find it. Do you see it, feel it?"

"I feel it. I don't know where." He struggled to focus on his surroundings, to focus on the energy tugging him like a taut rubber band that might break any second.

Nina picked up her flashlight. "There are several fingers that lead off the main cavity," she said, her voice lifting. "I searched the cave system as thoroughly as I could, but somehow I missed the other stone." She pointed in the direction of the shafts leading off the chamber. "One of them was so low, I had to crawl through it." She didn't sound as if she was looking forward to searching it again. "I had to chimney up another one, but it led nowhere."

Riley moved toward the one shaft she hadn't indicated. "Where does this go?"

"Nowhere. It doesn't go far. The skeleton—the pilot—is in there."

Energy drew him, buzzing through his veins.

Nina was still talking, but he couldn't hear her anymore. There was so much energy flooding him, he could hardly feel his own body, but it didn't matter. He entered the passage, stopped as his light hit the pilot's remains.

The body was heaped to one side, the leather jacket eaten away, the other clothing shredded nearly to dust and fallen away to expose bones. He directed the light at the skull. The remains revealed some kind of crushing blow to the head. He lifted his light, scanned it along the cave walls. He moved, walking around and stepping over the pilot. Not thinking, just reacting, just allowing himself to feel the heated pull that had his veins popping with fire, he smoothed his hands over the stone. Energy sparked against his fingertips.

A slight ridge in the rock sent him staggering backward. Visions tumbled wildly and he couldn't process them, they flooded so quickly.

He thought of the vision he'd seen as he'd entered the cave, the shadowy figure and the stone. The water, fire and quakes in his visions could be the evil the stones could unleash, the horrendous natural disasters, but what of the figure? He was seeing the stone itself. He was designed to see evil, terror, and the stone itself held that terror. It had been used for evil purposes at one time.

Nina's words came back to him. The shamans could use the stones for good as well as evil.

"Riley?"

He turned. Nina came toward him into the alcove. "What is it?"

"It's here."

Her face looked pale, but her eyes shone, confused and excited at the same time. "Here?"

"Maybe he knew someday someone might look for the stones, even find them. He didn't want them to find the twelfth stone." He glanced down at the pilot. "Even accidentally."

Nina came closer. "But there's nothing here. Nothing but…him." She slid past the bones, reaching down the far wall as if to remind Riley that the path came to an abrupt end.

"No!" he shouted, grabbing hold of her.

She turned, eyes rounded. "Why?"

He fought with the energy searing his mind. The visions he was having were too powerful, too fast.

He'd never been so close to a source of evil before, and he was afraid he could actually lose consciousness. His head felt as if it were burning up.

"Get back."

She obeyed, then gasped as he reached down and lifted the cold, dry femur bone of the corpse at his feet. Waves of blackness rolled over him and he struggled to keep his eyesight focused on the present.

"What are you doing?"

"Farther back," he ordered hoarsely.

His pulse rocked as he jabbed the tip of the bone at the raised area on the cave wall, then dropped it as a blur of something came at him. It was all he could do to leap sideways, pressing himself against the rock. A cavity opened up and he lunged, swept his hand into it. Something hard met his grasping fingers. He heard Nina screaming.

The mallet of stone crashed back. He flattened himself again against the rock, feeling its cold kiss as it swung by then slid seamlessly into the rock face.

All he could hear now was blood roaring in his ears.

He stumbled out of the alcove blindly, crashing into Nina.

"Oh my God," she breathed. "Oh my God, are you all right?"

He opened his palm. A small, unevenly shaped stone fell out of his hand. Blackness swallowed him.

* * *

Nina knelt over Riley where he'd fallen. The cradling dark of the cave enveloped her as her flashlight fell to the side, forgotten. She gripped his solid shoulders. "Riley!"

He was breathing. His chest was moving. Relief and fear tumbled down her veins. She ran her hands over his body, searching blindly for some sign of injury. Had that swinging rock hit him somewhere? She couldn't begin to wrap her mind around the idea of that mallet coming out of nowhere and disappearing back into the rock.

If she had ever doubted there was some unnatural power to the stones and the shamans who had held them, it was gone now.

"Wake up," she begged. She couldn't find any evidence of an injury. She kneeled over Riley, touching his face again. His lids fluttered. She leaned close. "Riley?"

He took a sudden, strangled breath. His eyes opened.

"Nina." Her name came out on a hoarse gasp. "The stone—"

"It's right here." She twisted, saw the stone where it lay several feet away in the narrow glow of her dropped flashlight, reached for it and stuffed it into her pocket.

"I can't touch it. You'll have to—"

A sudden explosion shattered the thick air of the cave. The blast came from the direction of the alcove where they'd removed the twelfth stone and rocked the hard ground beneath them. Fragments of rock and dirt rained down on them as the entire cave shook.

"Run," Riley ordered, staggering to his feet and pulling her up with him. "Get out of here."

Horror gripped Nina's heart. The rock floor swayed beneath her feet as debris continued to pummel them as if the cave were about to implode.

Buried. They were going to be buried alive.

She couldn't breathe or think or see. Her flashlight was lost in the nightmarish blackness. Powerful arms grabbed hold of her, dragged her, pulled her low, and pushed her through the crevice and out onto the ledge behind the waterfall.

Riley crawled out behind her. "Run!" he ordered again.

She didn't stop to ask questions, just gulped in the damp, oxygen-rich jungle air, and ran, racing across the rocks so fast she barely felt her feet touch them. She felt as if she were flying in a blur, sounds of exploding rock still filling the air behind them. The jungle clawed at her as she pushed her way through the tangled vegetation, not caring that the branches and vines whipped and scratched at her face and arms.

Her chest boomed painfully as she finally fell to her knees, exhausted and choking.

"Nina!" Riley reached her, dragged her up. His fiery gaze sent more fear thumping into her blood. They both stood there, stock still, listening over their harsh breaths.

"What was that?" she gasped. Her head felt light; her entire body trembled.

He reached for her face, held her jaw in his hard hands. "Are you all right?"

"Yes. I'm fine. Are you?" She remembered how he'd blacked out in the cave after he'd taken the stone.

"The other stones—" He stopped, steadying his breathing. He ran his hands down her shoulders, her arms, as if making sure she was really all right. "The other stones weren't hidden that way, were they?"

She shook her head. "Not like that. Not booby-trapped. How did that—" That mallet. How had that happened? It seemed impossible, but it had been real.

"They didn't want anyone to find the last stone," Riley said. "They made sure that if someone did, that person would die. And if he escaped the mallet, he would be buried alive."

Nina shivered. "How did you know?"

"There was energy in the rock. I didn't know, I just—I felt the stone. I knew it was there, and I knew it had to be hidden in the rock somehow. I think the pilot must have come across it accidentally."

And died. Oh God. That explained the damage to the skull.

Then he swore. "My pack is in the cave. The satellite phone." They were on their own, out of contact with his agency.

He grabbed her face again. "If anything had happened to you—"

His eyes shone with desperation. She knew the feeling. If anything had happened to him, she wouldn't have been able to bear it. And they still weren't home free.

But what would happen once they were? Last night had been a revelation to her, but anything permanent hadn't been in the deal. Maybe she hadn't had the right to change the rules, expect him to settle down with her. She could hold him with sex alone, maybe for a while, or at least she could try. But she didn't know if that was enough for her, not anymore.

"Nothing happened," she said, feeling her throat fill with emotion. "I'm okay." She could feel his hands on her face, shaking. Then it wasn't his hands she felt, but his mouth, crushing hers. It was a desperate, seeking, claiming kiss. His possessive, hungry mouth devoured hers and time stopped.

Until from somewhere near, a gun was cocked.

Chapter 15

"I hate to break up this tender moment, but you are going to hand over whatever you found in that cave. Now."

Avano's eyes gleamed in the jungle shadows. The deadly end of his gun pointed straight at Riley's heart as he tore his mouth from Nina's.

Nina's breath caught and he heard her whisper Avano's name in a shocked gasp.

"Throw that gun down," Avano ordered roughly. "And don't try anything stupid. I'm desperate and if I have to kill her and you, I'm not going to lose any sleep over it."

Nina's eyes burned huge and wide. Emotion

seared him and he focused on his training. Cooperate, bide his time, wait for a moment of weakness to strike. He couldn't save himself, much less Nina, if he was dead. Slowly, carefully, he moved his hand, slid down the shoulder holster that held his gun, let it drop to the ground. Nina had a knife tucked in her boot, as he did, and he prayed she wouldn't go for it.

"What are you doing, Richard?"

"What I should have done in the first place," the museum director declared. "I'm going to take the credit due to me. This time, it'll be me who gets all the media attention. Me who gets all the fame. How dare you come back to El Zarpa after what you did?"

"What I did?"

Tension speared Riley's body as he watched Avano turn the gun on Nina. She faced him with her head high, courage in her pale features.

Coward, she'd called him in the hotel this morning, and he suddenly wished he could take back that entire conversation. She'd had the guts to tell him that she loved him and he'd let her hang out on that limb alone. He loved her. Why the hell had that been so hard to admit? *You have to love someone for them to be able to hurt you.*

That was nothing but a crock of crap. He didn't love Richard Avano, and the museum director was about to hurt him more than anyone else ever had in his entire life if he killed Nina.

"You destroyed me, *Dr. Phillips.*" Avano's patrician features no longer resembled those of an elegant society don. He looked like a madman. "You turned me into a nonentity at my own museum. Everyone was talking about *Dr. Phillips* and her miraculous find." Every time he said *Dr. Phillips,* he spat out the name derisively. "I'm the one who had the vision, the foresight, the wisdom to approve the expedition. But did I get any of the credit?"

"I didn't want credit! It was the board who insisted on taking the discovery to the media. I never wanted—"

"It didn't work out quite how you wanted, though, did it?" Avano's silver-blue eyes were fiery. "You're ruined now, aren't you, Nina?"

"That's why you brought the hoax theory to the El Zarpan ambassador," Riley cut in.

Avano swung on him. The hand holding the gun trembled. He was a museum director, not a professional, and he didn't know how much it took to kill a man.

"Found that out, did you?" Avano rasped. "I was thinking I could let you live, but maybe not. I had it all set up. Dr. Phillips was discredited. Then she had to be a perfect idiot and ruin me all over again by stealing the stones."

"I didn't steal the stones!" Nina cried sharply. She took a step toward Avano and Riley gripped her arm, stopped her.

"Liar." Avano's blazing eyes ripped back to her. "How stupid do you think I am? A ghost didn't walk into the institute and take out those stones. Even the police don't believe there was an intruder. You think I do, knowing everything else you've done to ruin me?"

"I never did anything to ruin you," Nina said shakily. "I don't know how you could think—"

"I'm not a fool, Dr. Phillips. I know how you talked yourself up to the board. I saw how you basked in the media attention. The darling of the anthropological world, that's our *Dr. Phillips,*" he spat. "What about me? What about my career?"

"You're the director of the institute!" Nina blinked, confusion mixing with the horror in her eyes.

"They were planning to offer the position to you, you lying, underhanded bitch! Don't tell me you didn't know that."

Riley saw Nina do a double take. "What?"

"I had to discredit you. But then a funny thing happened. I didn't get any of the credit for the find, but I got plenty of the blame for the hoax."

"It backfired on you," Riley guessed. Served him right. Avano deserved to roast in hell for what he'd put Nina through with those hoax charges. He had to restrain the urge to lunge for the man's neck.

Keep it pointed it at me, bastard, he pleaded silently. Every word that came out of Avano's mouth convinced him further that the museum director wasn't planning to let them walk out of this jungle alive even if they handed over the stone.

And even if Avano let them leave alive, handing over the stone was too dangerous. Avano's personal greed and jealousy were nothing compared to the evil of the terrorists' plans.

"I have to save the museum's reputation," Avano hissed. "I have to find some kind of proof in those damn caves of yours. I stole the map from your files several days ago. I got the El Zarpan government's permission to come down here. I can't take anything out of the country, but they're going to work with me. Me, Dr. Phillips! Not you. Only me. The credit will be all mine this time.

"But your damn map is no good. If I hadn't heard that explosion... You found something, and you blew up the cave when you left. Making sure the glory's all yours again, right, Dr. Phillips? Did you find some evidence to back up your claims about the stones? I don't know how the hell you got him to help you, but even the police department thinks he's crazy, I know that."

"You're right. We found something," Riley said

before Nina could speak. He could feel the heat of the stunned glance she shot at him. "But I guarantee you that you don't want it."

"I'll be the judge of that." Avano's eyes lit possessively. "Hand it over."

"It'll get you killed," Riley went on steadily, watching the man's eyes. The weapon was a six-shot Smith & Wesson revolver. He'd only have to take one hit before he reached the man. "It'll probably get us killed, but we don't have a choice. You've stepped into something way over your head, Avano. Step out and you might get to live."

The only chance that either he or Avano wasn't going to die here in this jungle in the next few minutes was to scare the living hell out of the man. He pinned his gaze on Nina, caught her frightened eyes, prayed she would understand what he was trying to do.

"He's right," Nina jumped in, the desperate edge to her voice clutching Riley's chest as she turned back to Avano. "The stones are real, Richard. They're real! And there are some very bad people who want them. A terrorist cell. And if they get their hands on the stones, hundreds of thousands of people could die. And they'll start with you if they find you and you have what we found in that cave today."

"Shut up," Avano spat. "Hand it over. I'm not an idiot."

"She's telling you the truth," Riley said quietly, boring his gaze on Avano's face, willing the older man's attention to him. "Did you kill Danny Emery?"

"He killed himself. It had nothing to do with the stones. Stupid fool was having an affair with that trollop Juliet Manet. Your assistant, Dr. Phillips. Perhaps if you were not so busy all the time thinking about yourself you'd see what's happening right under your nose."

"What?" Nina shook her head. "Danny Emery and *Juliet?*"

"Emery was murdered," Riley corrected grimly. He had no idea why Avano would think an affair with a research assistant would cause the security chief to commit suicide. "The native guide who led Nina to the caves originally, he's disappeared. Nina's apartment was ransacked. She was attacked last night."

"She made it up. Everyone knows Dr. Phillips will do or say anything to save herself." Avano didn't seem to grasp the sick irony of his charge. "Now she's ruined herself by stealing the stones in her pathetic attempt to sidetrack attention from the hoax charges. I'll be the one to come back with new evidence. I'll get the acclaim I deserve."

"You'll be dead," Riley warned him. "What if Nina didn't steal the stones? Think about that, Avano. Nina didn't steal the stones. Someone else stole the stones. Someone else tore through her apartment.

Someone else attacked her, killed Emery and did God knows what to that poor El Zarpan native. What do you think is going to happen to you if you show up with another artifact?"

Avano gave a bark of eerie laughter.

"You're not making sense, Tremaine. You and Dr. Phillips came here to find something in the cave. You're not afraid of taking it back with you. You claim it's going to get you killed. Well then, you should be happy to hand it over. I'll take the risk for you. Oh yes, and the reward. What did you find? Another stone?" His eyes lit with greed. "Give it to me!"

"There were twelve," Nina said starkly, her eyes pleading with the museum director. "They only have eleven. I only knew there were eleven. But they'll figure out they need the twelfth, if they haven't already. They'll find out you have it. They'll kill you for it, I swear."

"I'd be more than happy to hand it over and see you die," Riley told Avano grimly. "But a lot of other people could die, too. The stones are deadly, Avano. They have power. Power that can wipe out hundreds of thousands of people in one fell swoop. We didn't set off an explosion to seal off the cave. That was just a tiny glimpse of the power of the stones. The shamans laid some kind of curse on the stones to try to keep them out of the hands of evil."

If Nina handed the stone over, Avano would kill them both. There was no reason for him to keep them alive. Their bodies could rot in this jungle forever without being found.

But Avano wasn't buying their story about the stones, about the terrorists.

"I've had enough!" Avano's hand shook again, his fiery gaze slashing back to Nina. "Give it to me!" he repeated, his voice echoing in the jungle stillness. He let loose a shot at Nina's feet.

Nina screamed and jumped back, slamming into a massive tree trunk. Riley lunged at Avano, stopping short as he saw the man stagger and drop.

Blood spurted from the side of his head, spilling out onto the thick viney undergrowth where he'd fallen.

"Oh my God," Nina whispered harshly. "What—"

Riley reached for her, fear coursing through his veins. Another shot tore through his right shoulder. "Run!"

There was no time. Soundless shadows moved from everywhere. A dozen figures, dressed in black fatigues and armed with guns, surrounded them.

One shadow stepped closer, into the slice of light in the dark canopy of towering trees. Nina's panicked eyes whipped from the figures to Riley. Blood soaked his shoulder, seeped down his arm. He could feel the ever-present tug of the stone she carried, and the fierce pressure of the figures. He fought the blinding images that exploded in his mind. He couldn't lose consciousness, couldn't leave Nina here alone.

The heat of the vision sucked him in. He didn't feel the bullet, the pain, the blood. He saw a dark mountain peak, knew the kiss of the cold air, heard Nina screaming as a robed figure aligned the stones—

He tumbled back into his body, staggered.

"We'll take the stone," Juliet Manet said. "And we'll take her, too." The men moved in on Nina. "Him," she jerked her head toward Riley, "we don't need. Finish him."

Chapter 16

"No!" Nina's heart slammed painfully against her ribs. She felt as if she couldn't breathe. Horror crashed through her as she saw Riley's grim, drawn face, the blood soaking down his arm, the men brandishing machetes and submachine guns. She rushed to place her body in front of him. "Don't kill him!"

Riley took hold of her with his good arm, stepped in front of her. His gaze blazed painful truth at her. He and Nina had been captured, and they didn't need him.

Juliet held a staying hand at the men with guns, her glossy hair slicked into a tight ponytail. Even in the jungle, she looked perfect and beautiful with her smooth olive skin and black, brilliant eyes.

"You will give us everything we want, Nina," she said with a cruel smile. "Don't be stupid. My father might even let you live. He's taken a rather sophomoric fancy to you. I find you rather annoying myself, but he seems to think you're pretty." She spat that last bit.

Nina's head reeled. "Your father?"

"Cristobal," Riley breathed harshly. "Her father is Eduardo Cristobal." Nina could hear the disbelief, the anger in his voice.

She caught Riley's gaze. His dark depths held that hollow, haunted look she'd come to know. He was fighting his visions and he was fighting to retain consciousness, whether from the wound or the power of evil surrounding them, she couldn't be sure. *Please don't leave me,* she willed him.

His eyes met hers with furious determination, but at the same time, she could see on his agonized face the toll his internal battle was taking. There was nothing either of them could do now. The explosion in the cave must have alerted their captors to their location. But the terrorists must have been searching here already. *They knew about the twelfth stone.*

Something deep inside Nina shattered. All she could do was fight for their lives as long as possible.

They were already out of contact with his agency since they'd lost Riley's satellite phone in the cave. But there would be agents waiting for them at the airport, and there were agents tracking Cristobal, closing in on him. If she and Riley could stay alive long enough, they might make it.

However long the long odds of any rescue were, they were better than no odds at all. She needed every ounce of hope inside her to fight.

"You planned all of this." She tore into Juliet, letting loose all her grief and anger. "You attacked me in the museum. You stole the stones. Danny—"

"Fool. He was going to go to the police," Juliet said. "What a fool he was. He had to be killed. He manipulated the security tapes so no one would know I was there that night. He was easy. You know how he always wanted to walk the women out to the parking lot. It didn't take much encouragement to turn that into something more. It was rather disgusting to have to sleep with him, but it was all for the cause."

"The cause to kill thousands of people? Juliet, do you realize what will happen—"

"Of course I realize, you idiot." She smiled her vicious smile again, and she was almost unrecognizable as the eager, perky assistant who had been at Nina's side for much of the past year. "But we're talking about people who deserve to die."

"Innocents," Riley broke in roughly. "Innocent people." There were still a dozen guns trained on his head.

"There are no innocent people in your country," Juliet snapped. She turned back to Nina. "When we couldn't make the alignment fit, we knew there had to be another stone. That stupid native guide should have told us, but he wasn't very strong and my father's men got a little carried away with the torture." She shrugged. "So he is dead. We caught up with you last night and tracked you here. How nice of you to find it for us. Good girl. Now hand it over. Maybe you can buy him a few more seconds of life, Nina. How sweet that you got together again with your little policeman. Too bad it won't end well."

Nina didn't want seconds. She wanted minutes, hours, years.

"Who killed Danny?" Nina demanded. "They know it wasn't a suicide. They know, Juliet. They know Manet isn't your real name. You're supposed to be in the Caribbean, but—"

"I had someone check in there last night under my name," Juliet said. "One of our people. I killed Danny myself, if you must know. And I liked it. I'd like to kill you, too, so shut up or I'll forget I'm supposed to let you live."

Juliet took a satellite phone from her belt and punched in a series of numbers. Using a global positioning unit, she gave their coordinates.

Oh God. They weren't going to the tiny scrap of an airport outside Los Mitos. The terrorists were coming for them here. The hope of rescue by the PAX agents who were to meet them at the airstrip died inside Nina.

She stuck her hand in her pocket. The stone felt heavy in her palm even though it was no larger than any of the other stones. She couldn't stop them from taking the stone, but if they hadn't figured out the alignment—

"Give me the stone now," Juliet ordered, putting the phone away.

Nina drew it from her pocket. The stone was similar to the others in design. There was a cloaked figure, arm outstretched, holding the stone. She knew the direction would match the final high peak in the Andean range. If her guess was correct, they could be anywhere along the magnetic lines and if the stones were laid out…

The power of the stones was no longer in any doubt.

But the bottom of the stone wasn't smooth, as she had expected. She turned it over. In the jungle shadows, she saw etched hieroglyphs. Like the markings on the other stones, it was as if they were lasered into the rock by modern tools. There wasn't as much varnish in the grooves, she realized at once. The hieroglyphs were newer, though still clearly very old. What did that mean?

Desperately, she focused on the etchings. Her heart hammered so hard, her chest hurt.

"Give it to me." Juliet's voice cut though her panicked study. "And kill him," she ordered the men.

"No," Nina cried, and she tossed the stone at Juliet. The younger woman caught it in her hands. "I'll give you the alignment, but only if he lives."

Riley's gaze flashed to her. "Nina, no," he said grimly, and she pleaded with him with her eyes to understand she was only trying to buy time. Her heart pitched hard at the emotion in his eyes. He understood, but he already believed he was as good as dead.

Cristobal's men stepped nearer. They were only a few feet away. She felt the rigid heat of Riley's body, and she knew he wanted nothing more than to strike out at these men, kill at least one of them with his bare hands before they, too, were killed. But he would never put her at risk.

"All right," Juliet said finally. "Let him live. For now. But make sure he's no trouble." She jerked her head at the man nearest Riley.

There was no moment of relief. Nina only had time to draw a jagged breath before the man behind Riley moved, slamming the butt of his weapon against Riley's head. A harsh sound came out of his throat, and he fell. Acting without thinking, she reached for the knife in her boot.

Juliet sprang forward and yanked her arm back so far that Nina saw stars. "Stupid bitch."

Dragging air into her lungs, Nina felt the cold kiss of a gun against her back. The knife dropped from her numb fingers. Juliet let go of her arm and in the same instant the man with the gun grabbed her hard against his body.

"My father will be very, very upset with me if I have to kill you," Juliet said. "And apparently you are going to be very, very upset if I have to kill your oh-so-good-looking detective. So I suggest you start co-operating. This isn't the institute, Dr. Phillips. I'm in charge now."

From the distance, the sound of a helicopter broke the thick air. Another of the men approached and ran rough hands over Nina's body, searching her clothes, she realized. They would be certain there were no more hidden weapons. Another man searched Riley's body, withdrew his knife.

"We're going back to the waterfall," Juliet said. "Move!"

Two of Juliet's henchmen grabbed Riley, treating his lifeless body like a sack. Muscles bulged from the terrorists' black-clad arms. These were trained, heartless killers, and her veins throbbed as she realized the odds stacked against her and Riley.

She wanted to fight. She wanted to kick and strike out at these men, at Juliet. Riley was already hurt, bleeding, out cold, and she was terrified they would leave him here to die despite Juliet's promise.

But with every minute that they both lived, there was still hope. She marched numbly, praying for this mystery agency of Riley's. Oh God, she didn't even know who they were, and they were her only remaining hope.

The sound of the chopper deafened her as they climbed the rise and reached the clearing above the waterfall. The helicopter made a vertical descent, lowering like a dark beast. Churning air broke the water into violent ripples as the helicopter landed.

Her heart pounded so hard, she became dizzy. The man still gripping her in his vise-like hands shoved her toward the chopper. She rebelled against his force, fear whipping cruelly through her. "He goes first," Nina shouted at Juliet. "Or I don't go at all."

Juliet's cold eyes sliced through her. Then she looked at the men holding Riley. Nina couldn't hear her voice, only saw her mouthed order.

"Take him."

The men hauled Riley into the chopper. Nina couldn't breathe watching his lifeless form. Then she was unceremoniously thrust in after him. Thrown into the cramped rear cargo area, she collided with Riley's cold body. She jostled into a sitting position, saw Juliet climb into the front and take the seat next to the pilot. The chopper's blades made a horrific whirring sound as it lifted off.

They had left the majority of Cristobal's men behind, she realized, to make their own way out of the jungle. Two climbed into the narrow rear seats even as the helicopter rose. They rested their guns against their laps, but their dark, deadly eyes watched Nina.

She could hear Juliet speaking to the pilot, but making out what she said was impossible against the roaring engine. Hazy sky swung around her, and she turned back to Riley.

Her palms cupped his still face. Her heart slammed painfully against her ribs. Swallowing against her uncomfortably tight throat, she leaned toward him, touched him, felt the rough side of his face where late-afternoon growth was already coming in.

"Riley," Nina cried. *Wake up,* her heart begged. He was a presence so searing to her, she couldn't imagine him dead. She half expected her fingers to burn when she touched him, but he felt cold, so cold. She felt his breath soft on her mouth, and tears scorched her cheeks.

Nina shifted to inspect his arm. There was nothing she could do about the bullet lodged there, but she could do something about the bleeding. Without a second's thought, she ripped at her shirt, tore it off and yanked the seams to pull off a sleeve. Quickly, she wrapped it around his upper arm, praying he hadn't already lost too much blood.

There was blood in his hair, trickling down the side of his face from where he'd been struck.

His head moved from side to side, and his eyes opened.

Breath choked in her lungs.

"Nina," he rasped.

"I'm here," she mouthed, knowing he couldn't hear her over the din of the helicopter. "Don't talk." She kissed him, her lips trembling, tasted the pain and grief in his mouth. "Just stay with me."

His eyes blazed, dark blue rimmed with haunting black. He would stay with her as long as he could. And when he couldn't, she didn't know what she would do.

If Riley's agency didn't find Cristobal before he demanded the alignment, there was no hope for either of them.

Cristobal's camp lay high in the biting winds of the Andes. They'd been transferred to a truck after the chopper landed—she'd caught something about mechanical problems with the helicopter, forcing them to continue overland. They'd been pounding on rough roads for hours by the time they reached the camp. The sound of the vehicle grinding to a halt was followed by booted feet and orders shouted in Spanish.

The rear cargo door of the truck slammed down

and Nina found herself staring into the barrels of half a dozen weapons. She reached for Riley. In the shadows, she could see his face drawn in pale lines, but he staggered to his feet, head high.

Beyond the men and the guns a stone building lay surrounded by barbed wire fencing. Torches spewed violent slices of light in the slashing wind. Stones were toppled on the corners of the building. Cristobal's camp had been created out of old ruins.

Here in these mountains, the lines of magnetic flux were enormous. All they needed to do was correctly align the stones—

Nina gripped Riley's hand tightly in hers.

A figure emerged between the men, who broke apart to make way. Juliet came around the side of the truck, searing Nina's eyes for a beat with the flashlight she held.

When she could see again, the figure stood before them. He was of average height, with a military bearing that was more about his rigid expression than his dress. He wore fatigues no different than the others, but he was in charge. He was strikingly handsome, just as Juliet was. His thick silver hair was slicked back, revealing a receding hairline. Strong features carved a cool face, dark eyes on fire as they laid claim to Nina.

"Daughter," he said, without taking his gaze off of Nina, his voice betraying no accent. "You have done well."

Juliet smiled, and for a moment Nina glimpsed the bright assistant she had known. Then the cruel twist came to Juliet's lips as she turned toward Nina.

"She insisted we bring him," Juliet said, nodding at Riley. She shoved the light at one of the men, and withdrew the stone from her pocket. "Here it is."

Cristobal took the stone quickly, weighing it in his hands, examining it carefully.

"Well done, Dr. Phillips," he said as he lifted his granite gaze again. He closed the gap between them, stretched out his hand in greeting. "Allow me to introduce myself. I am Eduardo Cristobal."

Nina went deathly still. She could feel the tension in Riley's grip on her fingers.

"You are a pretty one," Cristobal said, seizing her hand from Riley's, lifting it to his hard lips. He pressed a kiss to the back of her hand. "I've waited so long to meet you." Nausea swelled along with an inescapable fear. She prayed Riley wouldn't surge forward and take the man by the throat.

"They're coming for you, Cristobal," Riley said.

Cristobal sneered. "You mean your PAX League?" he asked blandly. "They haven't found me yet. But I found them, didn't I?"

Nina gaze slammed at Riley's stark profile. PAX League? The PAX League was a charitable organization dedicated to global peace and environmental missions. What was Cristobal talking about?

Riley didn't move or respond to Cristobal's charge.

"I guessed you might be one of them," Cristobal went on, "when I learned you had left the country with Dr. Phillips. I nearly destroyed your PAX League a year ago. Do you think I fear them now?"

"You should fear them," Riley responded quietly. "It will go all the worse for you if we're dead when they find you."

"They will not find me. They had a man inside one of my cells, but he's been taken care of now."

"They're looking for you now, Cristobal. The full force of the agency will hunt you down and destroy you. And if you use these stones— They *will* find you, Cristobal. Perhaps tonight." Riley lowered his voice in deadly warning. "If I were you, I'd get in that truck and get a head start."

"Ah, but you are not me, are you?" Cristobal reached out again suddenly, took Nina's chin in his harsh hold. "But I can be you, can't I? I will have your sweet Dr. Phillips."

Riley's arm, the uninjured one, swung out, but before it could connect with Cristobal, the man standing behind him grabbed him, yanked his arm behind his back while another stepped up to shove the butt of a gun against his cheek. Pain racked Riley's features, and his strangled grunt made Nina despair.

"I'll be gentle with her," Cristobal whispered as

he moved his gaze from Riley to Nina again. "Never fear. Now, take them."

Another man grabbed Nina's arm. She glanced back wildly for Riley. He was shoved forward, stumbling and then righting himself. His glazed eyes met hers for a second before she was jerked around by the man holding her.

The march into the night was short, and Nina wanted to scream with hopelessness. She stumbled once and a gun jabbed into her back. The sky yawned black overhead, broken by a thousand pricks of light. The dark peaks of the mountaintops spread out below in preternatural glory.

They were on a high plane, and the wind cut harder here. Boulders, some tumbled to the side, some upright, stood in an eerie circle. Cristobal's men spread out, flanking the boulders, their torches casting violent, flickering gashes of light, leaving her and Riley near the circle's center. She shivered in her thin T-shirt, her long-sleeved shirt having torn apart to staunch Riley's bleeding and its remains left behind in the chopper. She hadn't eaten since the morning break during their jungle trek, and she felt faint with hunger and panic.

"My dear Dr. Phillips," Cristobal said, his voice rising, eager as they stopped on the mountaintop. "This is a sacred place to my people. The ancients set up this temple, moved these stones into place.

From here, they harnessed the power of the universe."

He stood before the altar. One of the men stepped forward, draped a long robe over Cristobal's shoulders, stepped back. Juliet took a bag and placed the eleven stones in a pile on the uneven surface of the hewn altar, then stepped back.

"I need to see the twelfth stone again," Nina demanded, mustering her courage and her last hopes. Her heart hammered in her ears. "I… I didn't have a chance to study it."

There were symbols there, and she didn't know what she hoped to find. A bitter, urgent fear thrummed through her veins.

Cristobal handed her the stone.

She cupped it in her cold hands, almost dropped it. It was hot now, as if it had been taken from a bed of coals. Her skin felt as if it were burning. Desperately, she rolled the stone over in her hand, stared down through the slanting, erratic torchlight.

The symbols appeared to be carved over one another, making it that much more difficult to decipher.

Cristobal began to chant in the language of the ancients. She forced her ears off the sound of his deadly voice and the whipping wind, struggling to make out the symbols, separate the lines in her mind's eye. *Evil. The hand of evil. If evil aligns the stone—*

She gasped and tore her gaze to Riley's, leaned

close to him. "The hand of evil," she whispered against the wind. Cristobal lifted his arms to the heavens, his chanting growing louder. "It's another layer of protection." The stone had been hidden, secreted in the booby-trapped hole in the cave, then protected further by the imploding cave. "If it was stolen, if someone made it out of the cave with the twelfth stone, they would die." Hope seared her. *If the stones are aligned by the hand of evil, the evil will be destroyed!*

She couldn't begin to logically process the supernatural spells of the stones. But if the stones held power, if the secret curses of the caves were true, if all of that was real, then this was real, too.

Riley's eyes pinned her and something horrible flared in them. His gaze shifted to the sky, then back to hers. He was praying for deliverance, for this mysterious agency of his to save them. But they weren't here.

Emotion choked her throat. These men were evil, but the enormity of the act she was about to take overwhelmed her. She would be responsible for their deaths by giving them the alignment. Would she and Riley be safe? The etched curse told her evil would die. She and Riley weren't evil. It was a risk, but they had no choice. If she didn't give them the alignment, they would kill Riley. And she would die, too, because she wouldn't endure one day as Cristobal's woman.

"It's our only hope," she mouthed desperately to Riley.

Wind crashed across the high plain. The scent of the flaming torches filled her senses, and the taste of fear filled her mouth. Cristobal's chants floated around them.

Riley's eyes went dark and flat. "Give them the alignment."

"Align the stones!" She felt a brutal jab in her back as Juliet returned. Riley lunged at Juliet and another of Cristobal's men jumped forward to jerk him back, hold him.

Cristobal's chanting grew louder. His eyes were closed, his arms uplifted, seemingly unaware of all that went on around him as he implored the universe to fill him with power.

She caught the reference to the United States in his words. Whatever cataclysmic disaster he was calling down, it was upon her country.

Hands shaking, Nina quickly moved the stones about as if arranging a puzzle. Once aligned, she held the twelfth stone out to Juliet and pointed. "There."

Juliet's eyes burned brilliant black, and she grabbed the stone greedily. Cristobal's voice stopped, and he lowered his wild eyes to Juliet.

"Give me the stone," he intoned.

Juliet passed the stone to her father. Cristobal

leaned forward and, with a loud exclamation, lowered the stone into place.

Then the sky exploded.

Chapter 17

The heavens ripped apart. Flames flew like ghosts, roaring past Nina's face, circling at unimaginable speed. Booming thunder rocked her ears, all but deafening her. She heard screaming, and realized *she* was screaming. The mountain quaked and she fell, hitting the hard earth with shocking impact. The violent, spewing world around her disappeared for a stunning beat.

Riley! Her eyes flashed open to the mad sight of clawing, sweeping fire eating up Cristobal's men like ravening lions, burning them up and spitting them out in black piles of bones. She saw Juliet try to run, but one of the flame-like flying figures drank her whole in one swift lunge.

Cristobal disintegrated into a heap of ash before her eyes. The stones laid on the altar danced and sizzled.

But Riley— The deafening thunder receded, and she crawled to the altar, pulled herself up on her trembling legs. Shooting pain rocked her head and her mind reeled.

Riley.

She turned, dizzy and stunned. New thunder filled the air, and horror leaped in her throat.

Then she realized it wasn't a horrific, supernatural sound. It was choppers. Choppers were coming! Riley's agency? Oh, God, she prayed, please be Riley's agency.

"Riley!" she screamed in the blackening plain as the fiery figures swirled higher and higher, leaving nothing but piles of bones where there had been humans only moments before.

New light tore down as the choppers filled the sky above them, lancing their searchlights down onto the plain. And she saw him.

Riley lay, slumped against one of the toppled column-like stones. Numb and horrified, she couldn't feel her legs as she ran. She could only feel her heart, exploding inside her chest.

She fell to his side, reached for him. "Riley!"

He didn't move. He didn't open his eyes.

"Riley, please." She grabbed his shoulders, felt the

fire of his skin. "Wake up!" He was burning hot. Her stumbling mind raced in fear. He hadn't been disintegrated. He hadn't been turned into a pile of bones like Cristobal and his men. "Riley!" She shook him again, sobbing. "You can't die! You're not evil. Only evil—"

Searing comprehension hit her so hard, she almost passed out. He'd told her to give them the alignment. She remembered that awful look in his eyes. He'd known.

Riley had been implanted with a device in his brain to connect with evil. And that meant… *Evil was inside him!*

"Riley!"

His body went sharply cold, the heat disappearing as if he'd been thrown into ice. And he wasn't breathing.

She didn't know when the choppers had landed, didn't know when the men had poured out, only knew that hands suddenly had gripped her shoulders, tearing her away from Riley. All she knew was that Riley was dead. All she could hear was her scream.

El Zarpa Stones Recovered.

The headline in the newspaper on her coffee table chilled Nina as she lay, cloaked in draped darkness, in her D.C. apartment. Emotion burned raw in her throat. Once she would have cared that the stones had been found. She would have cared that the El Zarpan government had taken them back. She would have cared that she'd never be able to study their mysterious origins again.

The PAX League had determined that the stones' power had been destroyed in that final violent curse of the shamans. They were nothing now but lifeless items, incapable of creating disaster ever again.

But all she cared about was that Riley was gone. She lay awake day after day, night after night, in her darkened apartment, heart bleeding not for the loss of the stones but for the loss of Riley. The PAX League had scooped his breathless body into a chopper that night, and she'd never seen him again. They'd told her nothing. The flight that night—from chopper to private military jet, to their headquarters in Washington, D.C.—was nothing but a horrific blur in her memory.

She'd quit the institute. It was in complete turmoil following the news that had come out of Avano's betrayal and fabrication of the hoax charges, Emery's murder and Juliet's secret identity. The world knew little of the truth behind that fatal night in Peru. A terrorist cell had been decimated by U.S. covert operatives, and the stones had been recovered. Cristobal was said to have been insane, that he'd believed the stones held some magic power which was, of course, ridiculous.

Only Nina, and PAX, knew the truth. The power of the stones had been real, and it wasn't any ordinary covert operatives who had come to her rescue.

Riley's secret power had saved the world, but in order to save her, he'd sacrificed himself.

The realization that he'd known that aligning the stones would not only destroy Cristobal but also destroy him haunted her every day. He'd thought, they both had, that the PAX League wouldn't get there in time. He'd known that the only human on that plain who would survive the alignment would be her. He'd given up any last feeble hope of his own survival to ensure hers.

If that wasn't love, she didn't know what was.

And it was too late. He was gone. For a few days, she'd hoped he'd lived on inside her, that they'd made a baby that night in Los Mitos, but it hadn't happened. She wasn't pregnant.

She'd relived every touch, every kiss, every moment of those last forty-eight hours with him and despite the anger and the agony and the fear of it all, she would have given anything to go back and live them again.

Her mother had been to her apartment repeatedly over the past two weeks, worried and this time unable to hide it or pretend that her daughter wasn't in trouble. Oh, she'd been cleared of the fraud charges, cleared of suspicion in the museum robbery, but that wasn't the trouble she was in now. Nina was in danger of falling into depression, even her mother knew that. She'd left her job, left her life, her mother insisted. She had to go on.

Go on to do what?

Her father had ordered her to return to the institute, return to her work, take back her reputation and career.

She had no desire to return to the institute, to regain her career or her reputation. She could care less what the world thought about her. All she wanted was for Riley to show up at her door, alive.

A knock sounded on her apartment door, and her pulse quickened.

She ran to the door, looked through the peephole. A man stood there. A man who was not Riley.

Sick, she pulled the door open. She was dressed in a wrinkled T-shirt and jeans, but she didn't care. Just taking a shower every day and getting dressed was all she could force herself to do in the three weeks since she'd lost Riley.

"Dr. Phillips?"

"Yes?"

"My name is John Dante and—"

"I remember you." He was the PAX agent who'd infiltrated Cristobal's men. He'd been found tied up, beaten, in the ruins that had been Cristobal's camp on that terrible mountaintop. He'd been present during her debriefing at the PAX League after she'd been flown back from Peru. After everything that had happened in South America, she'd been beyond shock at the secret of PAX, for which Riley had worked.

"Chief Beck would like to see you today," Dante told her. His even tone was polite, his carefully guarded eyes unreadable.

"I've told you everything I know—"

"He sent me here to escort you." His firm words and steady gaze suggested she had no alternative.

"I don't want to go anywhere today." Maybe she didn't ever want to go anywhere. She was depressed, and she was wallowing in grief. Didn't anyone get that? And if she stopped grieving, that would be like letting go of Riley.

"I'm afraid I must insist, Dr. Phillips."

Irritation laced her veins. "What is this about?"

"May I come in?"

Nina rolled her eyes. More top secret stuff. She was all done with top secrets.

She let the agent inside. He shut the door and faced her. "We believe there is a possibility there are other pre-Columbian antiquities even now housed in museums inside the United States that may be prey to terror if they also hold supernatural powers. We need your knowledge, your skills, your experience to study these objects. We need you, Dr. Phillips."

Immediate denial sprang to her lips. "I—"

"The world needs you, Dr. Phillips," Dante said. "People's lives could be at stake. We need someone with your specialized skills in the League."

Need. They needed her. A small burst of adrenaline touched her pulse.

Riley had believed in the PAX League's cause. He'd died for it, too. If it was true, if she could save lives…

She felt hot tears swell behind her eyes. Riley's life couldn't be saved.

"Speak with Chief Beck," Dante said. "You won't regret it."

Crazy. She would be crazy to take one step out of her apartment with this secret agent man and step into the world that had been Riley's. But with every quickening beat of her heart, she knew she wanted to be in Riley's world. She wanted to save lives. She wanted a reason to live and a way to go on that would mean not letting go of Riley.

It took her five minutes to change her clothes. Another twenty and Dante was utilizing some kind of biometric security and sweeping her down into the depths of the PAX building, escorting her down a long corridor to Chief Beck's office.

"I don't know why I'm here," she told the chief when Dante left her there alone with Harrison Beck. "I mean, I know what Dante said. He said you wanted me to come to work for the League. But I don't know why I came."

"You came because you know what can happen without the skills and knowledge of people like you," Beck said. He stood, came around the desk. "We need you, Dr. Phillips."

She blinked against the rush of unexpected emotion. "I needed Riley. And he's dead now because he worked for you."

"Agent Tremaine lived well over another year because of the League," Beck pointed out. "And he believed in our mission."

Nina's heart fisted inside her.

"I know," she said quietly. "I believe in it, too."

There, she'd said it. She was not going to walk away. Not when lives could be at stake. Not when she could make a difference.

"There are many things we will need to discuss, Dr. Phillips, but first there's something I must show you." Beck took her arm and led her out of his office. "What we do here is highly classified and highly experimental." He continued speaking as he led her down first one corridor, then another. "When Agent Tremaine first came under our care, his life was over. He would have had no chance of survival without the device we implanted in his brain."

"That device killed him," Nina pointed out. "It was evil."

Beck nodded. He stopped as they reached a door marked Laboratory 31. "The evil inside that device was affected by the curse of the shamans, that's true. But he wasn't disintegrated like Cristobal and his men." He leveled his suddenly kind eyes on Nina. "When we implanted the device the first time, we had no idea if he would survive the operation. He spent months here in our laboratories in recovery."

Riley had been here, not in some foreign clinic. Of course. She should have known that.

Then she realized what he'd said.

Blood pounded in her ears. "What do you mean, the *first* time?"

"We had no idea whether reimplantation would save him," Beck said. "Or if recovery would be faster or slower. We're sorry to have kept this information from you, but until we knew—"

Nina had the sudden, almost uncontrollable urge to grab the PAX chief by the throat and demand information.

"Did it?" she breathed, a sob catching in her throat. If he was giving her hope where none existed…

She would kill him, that was all.

"Did it save him?" she demanded.

Beck turned the knob, pushed the door open. "See for yourself."

The laboratory lights were low. She heard the door shut behind her and she turned away from the tables, workstations and equipment to see a hospital bed against the wall.

And in the bed lay Riley, eyes closed, connected to about a thousand tubes and wires, a plain sheet draping him at the waist. The sight nearly sent her to her knees.

He looked pale, but alive! *He was alive.* Emotions ripped through her and her feet flew across the room. She could scarcely believe this wasn't a dream. She lay against his bare muscular chest, heard his heart beat strongly and then—

"Nina," he whispered her name and she looked up into his clear, dark, beautifully alive eyes. His head had been shaved and new growth had begun to cover the small scar where they'd operated. His wickedly handsome face was the same—carved, hard, intense and so overpoweringly male—that she could hardly breathe looking at him.

He moved his arm, wires attached to his wrists, to hug her closer to him and she crushed his mouth with hers in a deep kiss. "Riley," she choked against his lips. "Oh God, you're alive." She was crying and she didn't care. Then she realized there were tears in his eyes, too.

"I told them I was going to break down that door, walk out of here with wires hanging off my body, if they didn't bring you to me," he said in his wonderfully low, sexy drawl. "They wouldn't even let me near a phone. I'm so sorry they didn't tell you I was alive and when I found out they hadn't—"

His tormented eyes sought hers. She could see the exhaustion written on his face, but he was alive and he would recover. Even now, his lean, mean body belied the wires and tubes connected to him.

"They kept me sedated until yesterday," he said. "I guess they knew I'd start fighting as soon as I came out of it."

Fighting—for her.

"I wish they'd told me, too," she said, her breath catching on a sob. "I think they thought you weren't going to make it." The PAX League had protected its secrets, as always. And God, she realized, if she had known he had been alive and then that he hadn't made it, it would have been even worse. But she still wished she'd known. "It doesn't matter," she said, pressing her shaking fingers to his mouth when he would have gone on. "You're alive."

He was alive and he'd asked for her. This time, he'd been hurt and he'd asked for her.

"Are you okay? Am I hurting you?" Guilt sliced her. She was sprawled on him and she started to lean back, but he tugged her close.

"I'll heal," he said. "And soon. The recovery has been faster this time. I need you, just you. I had to see you, Nina. I had to feel you in my arms. That's all I need now."

"I love you," she said, half sitting on the bed beside him, still unable to take her arms from around him. She was inches from his eyes, and she wouldn't let go of that shining gaze. "I love you and I don't care what you say about your stupid top secret agent job anymore because I'm an agent now, too. I'm a PAX agent." The sudden swell of pride in her chest made her realize for the first time that she actually wanted this job. And she wanted Riley. And she'd be damned if she'd let him push her away now.

"I know," he said and she saw pride in his eyes, too. He wanted her to work with him in the League. He respected her strength, and she'd proven that strength to him in South America. But that wasn't what mattered to her most now.

"I refuse to lose you again," she announced. "You can say whatever you want, but I'm not budging. When you get out of here, you're moving into my apartment. Or I'm moving into yours. Either way. And you can just—"

He cut her off by dragging her head down and swallowing her words with another steaming, fantastic kiss. She could feel his body, hot and hard, beneath her. He wasn't *that* weak! Then she couldn't think because he was kissing her brainless.

"Would you shut up," he whispered against her

mouth when he finally let her come up for air, "and let me say something?"

Her heart popped as she saw the look in his eyes. Honest and clear and full of emotion.

"Well?" she breathed when she could speak over the lump in her throat.

"I was a fool that morning in Los Mitos," he said. "I was a fool a lot of other times, too. I was afraid of loving you. I was afraid—" He shook his head, his searing gaze tight on hers. "I didn't know how to love or be loved. Nina, I love you, more than I knew it was possible to love." He spoke the words in a burst, as if they were exploding out of him. "I don't want to live without you. I want to marry you, Nina. If you'll have me. And if they hadn't brought you here today, I would have broken out of here like a madman—"

Then he was the one who couldn't finish.

"*Have* you?" she whispered, her voice thick. "Are you kidding? No picket fences, though. Not for a while. We have work to do. You and me."

"I'll show you work," he growled and those wicked dimples she'd missed so much winked in his lean cheeks.

And she laughed for the first time in weeks, laughed when she'd thought she'd never laugh again. Then he pulled her tight and kissed her, loved her. She tasted desire and hope and the future they would share together just as soon as he could go home.

Then she realized she was already home.

In Riley's arms.

* * * * *

Don't miss DEEP BLUE, the third story in Suzanne McMinn's PAX LEAGUE *miniseries. Available in February 2006 only from Silhouette Intimate Moments.*